A DARK HALLOWEEN ROMANCE

CLOSE *To* MIDNIGHT

CARIN HART

*For those who love the idea of being chased through the night—
but who can't wait to be caught because you know what will
happen when you are…*

PLEASE NOTE

Thank you for checking out *Close to Midnight*!

This is a Halloween dark romance novella that is short, spicy, dark, possessive, and simply perfect for the spooky season! Each chapter is designed to point to a specific time during one very special Halloween for the heroine, and though this a M/F dark romance, there will be one chapter in the hero's twin's POV. I just want to state up front that there is no sharing in this series, but if you like the sneak peek inside of Nicholas's head, he'll be getting his own heroine in my upcoming Christmas novella.

Close to Midnight does include: an obsessed masked man who moonlights as an annual serial killer (though the heroine is never in any danger from him), minor blood/knife/breath play, a very primal chase through the woods that is portrayed as a "game", on-page murder (and mentions of prior hunts/kills), domestic violence (not from the hero), dubcon (and a hint of purposely mistaken identity), and explicit graveyard sex scenes.

If that's something you feel comfortable reading, please enjoy!

xoxo,
Carin

COME OUT, COME OUT,
little doe...

SALLY

From the moment I walked away from my old life and started a new one in the small town of Shadowvale, I learned there were three rules I should follow if I wanted to survive—

One: don't go outside at night alone.

Two: don't ask questions about the haunted house on the far side of town.

And three: don't catch the attention of either Reed brother, especially Hunter.

Me? I broke all three almost immediately.

It was by accident. I didn't understand why my co-workers at the coffee shop where I work thought I was crazy for walking to and from my job every day. It's not like the small town is dangerous. Its charm and its strangely low crime rate were why I left big city life for a small apartment in a tiny town I'd never heard of before. There shouldn't be any reason why I couldn't go outside alone, and I inwardly ignored that first unspoken rule.

I didn't have a choice. Thanks a Latte, the hipster café that was the only place to hire me on the spot without references, is about a six-block walk away from my apartment. It would be a waste of my check to pay for a ride when I can walk, and it's not like I was about to tell them that I didn't own a car anymore when I first moved to Shadowvale, thanks to my bastard of an ex.

Kinda hard to keep any assets when he cleaned out our joint account after scamming me into paying his way the last year and a half while he was cheating on me…

I do have one now, all thanks to Hunter Reed himself. Because, despite that third unspoken rule, I accidentally bumped into the town legend one night on my walk home and—though I'm not so sure why—I seem to have caught his attention.

My co-workers speak of Hunter Reed and his older brother, Nicholas, like they're ghosts or something. Between them both, they own the two biggest businesses in Shadowvale, as well as the massive haunted-looking mansion that overlooks the far side of town. They're untouchable here, and there's always a whisper of fear and excitement whenever someone mentions them.

I expected them to be powerful moguls in their fifties or sixties, real grandpa-types. I couldn't have been more wrong. That's probably why, when I first saw the good-looking guy in his late twenties/early thirties with sandy brown hair, amused blue eyes, a smirk that had my heart fluttering, and a body undeniably made for sin, it never occurred to me that he'd be a Reed.

Or that, after I accidentally bumped into him lurking around the back of Thanks a Latte with his hands in his jeans pockets and his muscular chest pushing against his black tee, I never thought he'd be *Hunter*.

When he eventually introduced himself, I thought he was fucking with me. Right after we met, the town bad boy insisted on walking me back to my apartment that first night. Smiling as he told me the same things that my co-workers did, that no one should be alone at night in Shadowvale despite the fact that he already was, he watched me closely for the whole walk, only offering his name when I was about to head inside my building.

I remember laughing nervously because I didn't believe him. I still gave him my first name back; not like it mattered since I'd forgotten to remove my name tag so he'd already called me 'sweet Sally' more than once in a teasing maner. I liked being with him, though, even if it was for only the small walk.

So, already too attracted to him for my own good,

I left him outside my apartment. I figured I'd probably never talk to him again, whoever he was, and kept my chance meeting with Hunter Reed all too myself.

Never see him again? I couldn't have been more wrong.

Because, about two weeks later, he walked into Thanks a Latte—and the whole café went quiet. Stacey and Noah held a quickly whispered argument about who needed to be the one to serve him, but his eyes sought me out.

He nodded, and I was standing in front of the cash register without even realizing I'd moved.

Hunter drinks his coffee with a splash of cream, no sugar. And I know that because, for four months now, I've taken his coffee order nearly every shift I'm on since he refuses to talk to any other employee but me.

Jasmine told me that a couple of weeks ago. As though one of the most powerful men in Shadowvale knows exactly when little ol' me is working, he doesn't come in when I'm off. But when I'm on? I can expect to see him at least once, and I've fallen harder and harder for the mysterious Hunter Reed every time I do.

I don't know why everyone is so afraid of him. In awe, yeah… I totally get that. But he seems… not nice. Hunter Reed is definitely not nice. But there's something about him that lures me in like a moth to a flame, and I know if he snapped his fingers, I'd follow him anywhere.

Too bad he seems to think of me as some silly little girl who needs to be protected from the big, bad world out there.

When he found out that the simple reason I walked home from work after every shift was because I didn't have a car, he told me about a guy he knew in town who would be willing to sell me one for a couple of hundred bucks. It's a beater, but it runs, and I'm grateful for the help regardless.

He forever asks me questions about myself, always deflecting when I turn them around, and anytime I suggest that maybe we could meet somewhere that isn't Thanks a Latte so that I could get to know *him*, he acts like I didn't.

Eventually, I had to get used to my disappointment that I'm way more into him than he's into me.

And why wouldn't that be the case? I'm just a wannabe barista in her mid-twenties with enough baggage to start my own department store who has a ridiculous crush on one of the most unavailable men in Shadowvale—

—until the other day, that is.

It was October 24th, a week out from Halloween, and Hunter waited until my co-workers inevitably gave us privacy—as they've done every time since they realized that he won't leave the shop until they do—so that he could invite me to spend Halloween night with him at his house.

It wasn't a date, though. Not like I thought it was.

It was a *proposition.*

Over the last few months, I'd learned a little about him. His favorite color is gray. He rides a motorcycle with a helmet that's branded with a skeleton's face on the shield and teases that that's why the gossips around Shadowvale call him Death; that's better than the other rumors I've heard that say the Reeds are serial killers whose private cemetery is full of their victims.

One time, with a sly smile, he told me he was into games. Like his name suggests, he's also an avid hunter, plus he loves to run, but his favorite thing to do is a game that—I'm pretty sure from the look on his gorgeous face as he tells me about it—only he knows the rules to.

I desperately wanted to play. Especially when Hunter bluntly told me that his favorite game ends with him and his chosen partner of the evening giving each other more pleasure than I could ever imagine.

I'm no virgin. Before Max, I'd had six other lovers, with half of them being drunken one-night stands I'd rather forget about. To be picked by a man like Hunter Reed…

Okay. So he doesn't think of me as a girlfriend type. He wants to fuck me, and I… I was okay with that.

And then he explained exactly what he would expect from me if I agreed.

Always a businessman, he offered me two thousand dollars to spend Halloween at his house with him. I could leave whenever I wanted and still earn the cash just for showing up, but if I stayed, I was looking at twenty-four hours where I agreed to do any and everything he wanted.

After what my ex pulled, I needed the money. Hunter has more than enough to share the wealth, and I didn't care that I was basically signing up to be a sex worker, trading the promise of my body for two stacks. I'd do it for free because this was Hunter, but I said yes because I get the idea that, if I argued about the money, he might have withdrawn the offer entirely.

So I don't argue. It's obvious to me that this wasn't the first time he found someone to keep him company on Halloween, or any other night for that matter. He brought the offer up almost casually, seeming like it wouldn't bother him one way or another if I refuse—but I still don't.

If I can only have Hunter Reed for one night, I'll take him for just that.

COME OUT, COME OUT,
little doe...

4:02 PM

SALLY

I'm halfway through my shift—my heart suddenly skipping a beat—when Hunter pushes open the door to the café. With a white clothing box tucked under his the arm, he stalks inside Thanks a Latte as though he owns it.

The way the Reeds seem to run everything in town, who knows? He might.

He doesn't wait in line. When the guest about to order sees him, the gentleman makes some excuse and hightails it out of the shop. Noah mutters he's going to go mop out the bathroom, while Kelsey busies herself with the coffee bean roaster.

Me? I only have eyes for that sharp jaw and the hint of stubble covering it.

As soon as he reaches the counter, Hunter holds out the box. "For you. For Halloween."

Accepting the box with a soft 'thank you', I ask, "Is it my costume?"

"You could say that. It's what I want you to wear."

For two grand, if he wanted me to parade around his room naked for the entire evening, I would. But if he wants me to wear something in particular, I can do that, too.

Lifting the lid, I peek inside. It looks more like a nightgown than a dress, all lacy and silky, and when I dip my fingers in, running them over the material, I can't help but murmur under my breath how nice it feels before putting the lid back on.

"Pair it with heels," he says, his words an obvious demand. "Don't worry about a coat. I'll make sure to keep you warm."

"I… Okay. Thanks, Hunter."

Leaning over the counter, he ghosts his thumb over the height of my cheek, not quite touching me. "Don't mention it, little doe. Did you make sure you're off tomorrow night?"

I nod quickly, not sure what has my pulse pounding louder, my pussy clenching tighter: this whisper of his skin over mine, or the nickname he just gave me. "Yes. Halloween and the day after, too."

His lips twitch. "Good girl."

My whole body flushes at the way he rumbles that. "I figured I might be tired by the 1st."

"Or maybe you'll be locked up in my house, never to leave it."

Behind me, Kelsey gasps, and I know that she heard that. I roll my eyes. Hunter's obviously teasing—and, besides, it's not like it would be so bad to be trapped with him.

"One more thing." Reaching into his back pocket, he pulls out a folded piece of paper. He slides it across the closed lid of the box on the counter. "The address."

Picking it up, I quickly unfold it. There's a single street address written in black ink on the scrap. It's not necessary. As if I didn't already know where Hunter Reed lives, only one oversized manor stands on the aptly named Reed Way: his family's.

He has a brother. Nicholas Reed, who I've learned next to nothing about since it's Hunter who the whole town seems to be wary of. All I know is that Nicholas is the one seemingly in control, and that Hunter and his brother are tight, though I've never met him before.

I won't tonight, either. Nicholas seems to have his own plans for Halloween, and it'll just be me and Hunter at his house tonight.

"I want you there by midnight on Halloween. Not a minute later. You'll park your car inside the gate. I'll have it open for you, then you'll follow the path behind the house. Wait for me there. You understand me?"

Breathless, I nod again.

His blue eyes darken as he looks at me. For the moment, it's like it's just the two of us, like no one else in the coffee shop exists at all as he says, "You'll like my game, Sally. I know you will. And I look forward to playing."

His game… he told me that I'll find out the rules once it's Halloween. Like I told him last week, as long as he doesn't physically harm me with the intent to cause me pain, I'm down for anything.

Hunter doesn't take his usual cup of coffee today. With one studying look at me, making me feel like I'm already naked, he smirks, then leaves the shop.

My co-worker hustles right over to me, her big brown eyes wide.

Kelsey grips my arm. "You're not really going to go up to that house on Halloween, are you?"

To be honest, I'd walk across broken glass for Hunter Reed if he asked me to.

"He invited me."

"And you can say no," she insists. "Sally… you don't know what goes on up there when it's Halloween. I've gone past that big house before. I've heard screams. It's not worth it."

If Hunter picked me out to be his playmate this Halloween and his previous dates were left screaming, I'm pretty sure it will be worth it.

He promised he'd never hurt me. I don't know

why I believed him when he solemnly vowed that I'd always be safe with him, but I did.

And if he turns out to be as big of a fucking liar as Max did, maybe I'll deserve to be another so-called victim of one of the Reed's.

Either way, I'm going tomorrow night.

And I can't wait, either.

COME OUT, COME OUT,
little doe…

11:45 PM

NICHOLAS

Our birthday is on Halloween.

Sometimes I wonder if that has something to do with the way my twin and I turned out. That we were always destined to be as dark as the shadows that lurk through our small town, all thanks to the day we were born.

But then I remember that we're Reeds. Since our great-grandfather came to Shadowvale, purchasing five acres of land to build our family home and the private cemetery he planned to house our remains forever, our bloodline has been tainted. Twisted.

Hungry.

Aster Reed buried his first wife out back—and the lover he caught fucking her while he was spending his days out of the house, running the local sawmill; well, after he was done at the mill, he buried the *pieces* of them. That wasn't his first kill, either, and he's responsible for more of the graves dotting our land than my grandfather and father put together.

Hunter and I turn twenty-nine at midnight tonight. A hundred years after Aster ruled Reed House, in a world much harder to hide our crimes, my twin and I are already catching up to his total.

We still have to be careful. Our reputation as Reeds—not to mention the family wealth—awards us some cover. Half of Shadowvale whispers how people who visit our land rarely return from it, while the other half are grateful that my great-grandfather's sawmill and the sanitation company our grandfather started back in the 50s still employs most of the town.

The businesses are mine these days. Technically, they belong to Hunter and me, but my twin doesn't have the... temperament to be the face of the company, even though—as identical twins—we have the same damn face. He prefers to hang back in the shadows, preparing for his annual hunts.

Unless he has to be Nicholas, of course.

But now that we're older and the thrill of the kill is something to savor instead of waste, one planned target a year is as much as we can allow these days without risking getting caught. One specifically chosen victim to satisfy his prey drive and my deep-seated need to be fucking *God*. I find someone who deserves to die and bring them here, and Hunter gets to hunt him down on our land. We trade off on who actually gets to kill, but aside from a few times that Hunter "had no choice", we try to keep our tally inconspicuous.

That's why we have three rules we abide by.

One: don't target a local.

Two: don't leave any witnesses.

Three: don't involve anyone else in our Halloween hunt.

Because, tonight, there will definitely be a hunt.

We were bred this way. *Born* this way. Two dark halves of the same twisted soul, on Halloween, we can be the monsters we are. The rest of the year, my charming smile hides just what I'm capable of. Hunter's smirk tells the entire fucking world exactly what he is, but despite the rumors, the warnings, and the whispers… there are still those who'd sacrifice *their* soul for one taste of him.

And that's precisely why, tonight, I'm giving Hunter free rein to break all three of our rules.

I'm the older brother. Born eleven minutes before Hunter, I also wonder if that's part of the reason my twin lives for the chase the way he does. Once he sets his sights on his target, there's no stopping him.

Except, it seems, for Sally Clark.

Four months now, he's been watching her. *Stalking* her. The sweet blonde barista who works at one of those generic cafés in the center of Shadowvale, she snagged his attention in a way different from all of his other prey.

Little doe. That's what he calls her. His little doe —and instead of wanting to hunt her down, he wants to make her his.

Only… I know Hunter better than I know myself. More than that, us Reeds know exactly what we are. It's the same reason that I refuse to allow Hunter to use his unique skills to find Tamryn Carlisle for me. A woman's warm body is good for a night, maybe two, but going back to Aster Reed being betrayed by his first wife, none of the men in our family ever *keep* them.

Hunter's different, though. I want to believe that I am, too. What I feel for Tam… if it's not love, then it's madness and obsession, and that's probably far more dangerous for the both of us.

To my twin, love *is* madness and obsession. And while he's had his fun over the years, I always knew that I'd have to be the one to fuck a willing woman and have her bear my child so that the Reeds don't end with Hunter and me before casting her aside. Because Hunter? When he gets his hooks in the woman who controls him, he will never, ever let her go.

Me? I've only ever wanted Tamryn. If I can't have her, I'll do what I have to, pretend anyone I do fuck *is* her, then let my dark side seep out whenever I can.

Again, we're Reeds. That's how it's always been, and how I'm resigned to believe it'll always be.

We never knew our mother. The woman who fucked Calvin Reed and gave birth to his twins on Halloween… whatever happened to her, she was gone before either me or Hunter could imprint on her face. Probably for the best since most of our dad's kills were women he targeted because they couldn't fight back.

We were twelve when we realized that there are monsters and there are *monsters*. That Halloween? Calvin became our first kill, and since then, Hunter's made it his point to slaughter men to balance the graveyard.

Since I agree, I pick out those who deserve it. Is it my way of making it up to a faceless mother I've never known? Or to prove that, maybe one day, I might be the kind of guy Tamryn deserves?

Or is it because there isn't anything I wouldn't fucking do for my twin?

Yeah. It's probably that last one.

Which leads me to tonight…

Just because I refuse to find Tam, when I discovered that Hunter was more obsessed with his Sally than I've ever seen him with anyone or anything before, I started to plan; that's what I do best, after all. Knowing he prefers the shadows, lurking outside of her apartment, watching her from a distance, I visited Sally during the day. I fucking hate coffee, and I drank enough of the stuff these last few months to just about piss brown, but I got to know her.

Well, *Hunter* did.

I smiled. I flirted. I did everything I had to to make her fall under my spell, making her fall for Hunter, knowing all along that she would be the best birthday gift I could offer my twin.

That's how I knew she was different. If she just caught his fancy, he'd fuck her and move on. The fact that it's been months and the real Hunter's only spoken to her once tells me that he already fucking worships this girl. He thinks he'd ruin her if he got the chance to touch her so he just chooses *not* to.

My twin would never bring her into our world. Into our darkness. Into our game…

But if I did? Well, that's a different story, isn't it?

He should've known something was up when I called him to meet me in the parlor that leads off into the backyard at a quarter to midnight. Our hunt always begins once it's dark on Halloween night, not the one before.

Tonight, though… Hunter deserves more than a few hours with Sally.

Besides, I have another hunt planned for tomorrow. Since taking Sally will only satisfy one lust, I can't deny Hunter his turn to kill.

And when I pass him the photo of this year's target, I'm sure I picked one to his liking.

"Oh, Nicholas." His eyes—the same shade of blue

as mine—seem to gleam when he recognizes the man in the picture. "And you arranged for me to hunt him at midnight? I can torture this fucker for hours, then finish him off tomorrow night. Just what a prick like him deserves."

I figured he'd agree with my choice. Especially since there are very rarely secrets between me and my twin. Though I've been careful to keep him from learning just how much time I've spent priming Sally for him, he's told me all about her. Everything he learned from stalking her both in person and online… everything he dreams of doing to her… how he'd lock her up in our house forever if I nudged him into thinking it was a good idea… I know it all, and I used it to help arrange this surprise for him.

If he can't have Sally, the best thing he can do is take his aggression out on someone who hurt his little doe. And I'll let him… but that's only one part of his gift.

Because the other part? Is that he *can* have Sally if he wants to.

Fuck knows she's more than willing…

I mirror his grin back at him. "Not tonight. He's still arriving at the house tomorrow after we have dinner. The hunt starts then."

Another tradition. Every year on our birthday, even before we got rid of our dad, we made sure to sit down to dinner together. We're closer than most twins, though not inseparable, and no matter how busy we are—with business… with the hunt—that time to eat it ours.

Then the fun can begin.

"Yeah? Then what's tonight?"

My grin widens. "I arranged for you to get laid."

He's obsessed with Sally, but I know Hunter. If I throw pussy at him, he'll take it, then head over to her apartment with some other chick's juices coating his dick without thinking twice. She's the one he wants, and I know he hasn't gotten any since he met her, but he's not going to go without so long as a willing woman is dropped in front of him.

Especially since he'll only take it if he can run it down first…

Two thousand for his Sally is a great deal, though he's had cheaper. I've found escorts who'll let Hunter run after them on our property for five hundred—and they usually offer to come back for a discount after they get a taste of one of the Reed twins.

It's even better that they never know who it is that's railing them. It could be me, it could be Hunter… and considering my twin has a mask kink, sometimes it's neither.

I swear, his mouth is already watering. Wiping it with his thumb, he crows, "A chase and a hunt. Fuck me. Am I dying or something? What's the occasion? Besides the obvious, I mean."

"Just because you deserve it," I tell him.

He accepts that answer easily, just like I knew he

would. "You arranged the girl. Tell me, who am I supposed to be tonight?"

I toss him the mask I'm holding in my hand. "Hunter."

"Good." My twin snatches it out of the air. "I like being Hunter the best."

Of course he does. When he's Hunter, he really allows himself to get into the chase—and, later, the hunt. Then again, when he's being me, he adopts this ridiculously snooty tone that no one ever seems to question which has me wondering if they're that afraid of me to point out I sound different... or if I really do sound like that after all.

"Any conditions?" he asks me next, already focusing on the chase. "Safe words? I hope you got that redhead from two years ago, Nicholas. She let me do whatever the fuck I wanted. Twice."

The redhead, huh? He says he wants her now, but just wait until he sees who I bought for him instead.

"It's someone new," I tell him, purposely staying coy. I fucking *hate* surprises, but my twin? He lives for them and I'm nothing if not obliging. "Just so you're aware, I booked her for all of Halloween."

That's what I paid for. Hunter? Once I set his little doe in his path, no way he won't take the bait and trap her the way he's dying to.

Poor bastard. He's purposely given himself blue balls for months, fantasizing over the one woman he won't let himself have. I almost feel bad for Sally.

When he finally gets her under him, I can't imagine he'll let her up for air for long.

He won't hurt her. I promised Sally that when I was Hunter mainly because I *know* my twin. He'd cut off his own cock before he hurt someone he believed earned his devotion and his protection. If ever there was prey perfect for him, it's his sweet Sally, and every moment I spent with her as Hunter only justified my manipulations.

My twin will understand. I couldn't care less if the girl did, but that's not my problem. She doesn't know Nicholas.

Except for Hunter, no one does—and I like it like that.

"Shit. And all I got you for our birthday this year is a Maserati to add to your collection." I already have seven sports cars, but it's the thought that counts. "You win, Nicholas, you got me fucking beat. How about this? We usually keep the cameras off when I get to chase my girls. You want to watch tonight, go ahead."

I've seen Hunter fuck plenty. It doesn't bother me. We don't share, and we got that mutual masturbation bullshit out of our systems when we were horny teenagers, so watching Hunter fuck his women is just like watching myself in a mirror. It's more narcissistic than anything else.

Now, keeping the cameras on for the hunt? Maybe we're begging to be caught, but we have a record for every Halloween night going back two decades. I never get off harder when I'm jerking it than when I watch the life go out of our target's eyes.

But his chases are as sacred as when I bring my women to the red room inside our home, and I would never ask him to leave the cameras on for one of those.

Still, I appreciate the gesture. Hunter has no problem with me seeing him fuck, either, and outdoor sex has always been his thing so there's always bound to be someone watching. However, he's never had a woman he's considered his before the way he does Sally.

I can watch Hunter, but my brother is too possessive to ever let me get an eyeful of her. I respect that, too, and I already anticipated it.

The cameras will be off this year, another present for my twin, and I tell him so.

Before he can ask me why, I change the subject back to tonight. "She wants the whole experience, Hunter. A full chase. No pain, but anything else goes."

That's the truth. Does he need to know that another Hunter already promised her that he'd fulfill any fantasy she had without her having to worry about getting hurt?

No. Of course not.

Hunter won't hurt her—but I can't say the same for our target tomorrow night.

As my twin pulls the full-hooded cloth mask on

over his head, I see the hunger in his eyes, the anticipation in the curve of his lips before it's covered by the skeleton's mocking smile.

Then, Hunter's husky voice only slightly muffled, he says, "Then that's what she'll fucking get."

COME OUT, COME OUT,
little doe...

12:01 AM

HUNTER

Do I have the best twin or do I have the best motherfucking twin?

This is just what I need tonight. Taking a page out of Nicholas's book, I can get my rocks off, fucking a new girl while thinking of my sweet Sally, and after that, me and my brother can take out the most perfect target he could have ever picked.

Damnit. I thought we would go all out for our thirtieth next year, but it looks like Nicholas figured he'd start the last year of my twenties off with a bang.

Literally.

I'm already hard. My dick's like a length of steel pushing against my jeans. Not so unusual, really. All I have to do is imagine Sally Clark with her big doe eyes, that short blonde do with hair so pale, it's almost white, and her body… fuck. She's built to proportion, with small tits, a flat ass, and a delicate shape. My own personal porcelain doll brought the fuck to life, if I ever laid my hands on her, good chance I'd break her.

I wouldn't want to. I'd do whatever the hell I could to keep her from shattering anymore than she already has, but I want to work my cock inside of her, hear her scream *my* name so badly that as much as I wouldn't want to lose control, who knows what would happen?

For four months, I've hungered for her. *Craved* my sweet Sally. Only knowing that she's too good for me and that, as a Reed, I'm not built to have a normal relationship kept me from taking her the moment I couldn't stop thinking about her.

This isn't just love. What I feel for her, it's obsession, something so dark and twisted that I'd rather go without than taint something so pure and *good* as Sally.

That doesn't stop me from going hard at just the thought of her. Like a stray dog marking his territory, I usually wait until I'm standing outside of Sally's place to nut, leaving my come outside as though trying to leave some clue that I'm there.

That I'm watching.

That I'm *waiting*.

This is Halloween. This is our birthday. For the

first time in ages, I'm not stalking behind my little doe, but that's only because Nicholas told me I needed to be home early tonight for my gift.

A little chase, a little paid-for primo pussy, and a hunt?

I don't give a fuck who Hunter hired. If she's here, she'll know what to expect, and I won't have to hold back.

It's not Sally—but, tonight, it's good enough.

My mask is in place. I have my phone in my back pocket in case Nicholas needs to contact me, and my knife in the holster strapped to my belt. I'm Hunter, my favorite Reed to be, and I'm so goddamn horny after four months without a hot cunt to sink my dick into that I might have to run the girl to the ground immediately just to get my first nut off.

Good thing Nicholas booked her for the whole night. I have a lot of pent-up aggression and need to work through, and this is my favorite way to do it.

Dropping my hand to my crotch, I cup my cock, squeezing it, enjoying the pleasure mixed with pain as it builds at the base of my spine.

Nicholas told the girl to wait for me out back. He wouldn't have invited her inside—not Nicholas, not with his history—but if he gave orders for her to be out there, I have no doubt that that would be where I'll find her.

And I do, though I freeze in the doorway when I see who is huddling on the porch, nibbling on her bottom lip, glancing up in worry when my big body fills the door frame that leads out to the back.

"Hunter?" My cock twitches to hear my name in her sweet, high-pitched voice. "Is that you?"

Oh, Nicholas. See how quick I can turn on a dime because, two seconds ago, I was thinking about what I can do tomorrow morning to one-up him for our birthday… and then this happened.

That *fucker.*

She gestures at her body. Draped in white silk, she's wearing a sleeveless white dress that barely hits her ass. The three-inch white heels she's got on would bring her up to my nose, closing the gap between us, though I'm more impressed at what they do to her legs.

Oh, fuck. I was already hard, but now I'm about to fucking explode in my pants.

She has no idea. As innocent as ever, she runs her hands down the silky material, tapping her hands against her thigh.

"This is the dress you brought down to the café when you invited me over," she says, oblivious to the fact that I'm basically already eye-fucking her from behind my mask. "It's a little shorter than I thought it would be, but it fits otherwise."

Oh, it definitely fits, but fuck if it doesn't leave me perfect access to that amazing body of hers.

Which the Hunter who bought that dress for her would've known all too well.

Only one thing: it wasn't *me*.

I haven't been back to Thanks a Latte since I first met Sally. It was too tempting to pretend I could be the kind of guy she'd want, the kind of lover she'd deserve; instead, I kept my visits to the dark, hiding in the shadows, becoming part of them as I watched over my little doe.

But if I'm not the one who visited Sally, who invited her up for Halloween, who managed to get her to agree to play with me tonight as someone inevitably did or else she wouldn't be here… it doesn't take a genius to figure out who *did*.

He'd say it wasn't lying. He's not wrong. I never came out and asked him if he was spending time with my Sally, pretending to be me. Looking back on it, it should've tipped me off, all those times he complained about his piss stinking like coffee, or how pushed me to watch over Sally at night while keeping me busy most days.

Logical bastard. If I wouldn't pursue Sally, he would—but he'd do it as me. He's done it before. I've done the same to him.

But our girls… they're supposed to be off-limits.

I don't go after Tam. He was supposed to keep his distance from Sally.

And Nicholas did, didn't he? Because he wasn't Nicholas—he was Hunter.

That's exactly how he'd see it, too. That I wanted Sally, that I would do anything for her except break her all over again like that bastard of an ex did, but it wasn't enough. I needed her, so he gave her to me.

Still…

"Don't move. I'll be right back."

She swallows, then nods. "Okay."

I turn around, pulling the door behind me before I start stalking toward the den where I left Nicholas.

I don't even have to get that far. Halfway out of the kitchen, he's right there—and he's cocking his head in my direction.

"Don't make all that fucking coffee I had to drink a waste of my bladder, Hunter. I got her here. I got her for you. What happens next… tonight's for you. Make it worth it."

"Shit, bro. I don't know what to say."

"I do." A grin tugs on his lips. "Happy birthday."

Beneath my mask, my lips mirror his. "Happy hunting."

He moves next to me, clapping me on my shoulder. "Happy fucking Halloween."

***

Less than a minute later, I'm back on the porch.

Thank fucking God she's still here.

Honestly, I can't even be pissed at Nicholas. I wanted to stay away from her, and I did, but now that she's here on Halloween…

All bets are off.

I just have to be careful. In control. I have to make the most of this night because, when it's over, there's a good chance she'll disappear the same way Tam did.

Unless I give in to my basest desires and—

Sally shivers as I step outside.

"Cold?" I ask.

"A little," she lies. I see goosebumps on her bare arms, her nipples poking through her light bra *and* the dress, leaving me a pair of targets to lock on as I loom closer. Her shiver becomes a tremble, head tilting up to look at me.

Her eyes widen. "I didn't know you would be wearing a mask."

"It's part of the game," I assure her. "I'm sure I told you that."

"Maybe. I know you said you love playing around on Halloween."

"I do. After all, that's why you're here. Isn't it, my sweet Sally?"

When her whole body jerks, I like to think it's from the way I drop my voice, purring for her instead of the midnight breeze surrounding us. I'm not so worried about her freezing in that skimpy dress. She'll warm up once she starts running, and when I catch her?

I'll make her nice and hot.

There is no remorse in me. No mercy. There never has been, and the most I could do was torture myself by watching over the one thing I couldn't

have for fear of ruining it. But now that she's here…
there's not a single chance in hell that I'll let her
walk away without taking what she so freely is
offering me.

After all, she wouldn't be here if she wasn't.

We have rules. When it comes to my chases, when
it comes to Nicholas's women, when it comes to our
hunts. What is life without structure, right? Especially
with such a logical business mind like the one that
belongs to my twin, Nicholas always enforces the
rules.

As for me? They do the job of keeping me in line
so I follow them—and even set some of my own when
it suits me.

It's been ages since I set a woman loose on our
property, but they've always been the same. After all,
what good is a chase if there isn't the element of
danger, the element of hope, and a prize for the
winner at the end?

I'm fair enough. Technically, all of our targets—
those we fuck, and those we kill—have a chance. Sure,
it's not like they'll be able to navigate five acres in the
shadows, avoiding all of the traps that Nicholas and I
set up to make it even more fun, and find the gate that
leads to freedom.

I do the same with my women, though they're
actually allowed to leave when I'm through with
them.

Our targets? Oh, no. Once Nicholas picks them

out, they'll end up as part of the Reed Family Cemetery.

There won't be any traps yet; I would never risk one of my girls triggering them by accident and my twin knows that. Tonight is all about hunting my prey down and fucking her wildly when I do.

She understands that. Before I even set her loose onto the rest of our property, I make sure that the other Hunter—when my twin was me—told her what to expect. That, wearing nothing more than that dress, she was going to play a little game.

"A game?" she echoes. "What kind of game?"

"Hide and seek."

"You mean… I hide and you find me?"

"That's right."

She leans toward me. "And what happens when you find me?"

Oh, yeah. I don't know what my twin did to put my little doe in such a thrall, but there's no doubt in my mind that she's here because she wants to be. She knows exactly the answer to that question, but I tell her anyway.

"Whatever I want."

She blinks, going still. "For one night, right?"

If that's what she thinks…

"My game has three rules. You ready to hear them?"

At her nod, I hold up my hand, extending one finger.

"One. If I find you… if I *catch* you? I get to do whatever I want."

"But you won't hurt me. You said that."

The other Hunter did, and he was right. I would never hurt my little doe.

"And I won't. You have my word. Now, two. If you find me, same thing goes. Circle back, track me down, I don't give a fuck. But if you see me before I see you, you can ask for anything except how to escape."

"Escape?"

Sweet, sweet Sally. My innocent girl.

"That leads me to the third rule. If you want to win our game on your own, you have to find the gate that leads out of here on the far side of the property. There's only one that will be unlocked, and if you find it, I'll double that amount I offered you."

I fucking adore this woman, but I'm not a fool. I also know my twin. To get her here, to have her dress up like this when it's maybe forty degrees outside at most, having her primed to fuck a masked man at the drop of a hat with only my word that I *am* Hunter Reed… he's paying her.

I'm not offended by the idea. In fact, this is what we usually do. This way, both us and our girls get something out of the exchange, no questions asked.

I never thought Sally would be one of my girls, but if the money makes it easier for her to agree, and

I can get a chance to work out what I feel for her… who gives a fuck?

If I thought she'd take a hand-out, I'd go to the bank right now and hand her as much cash as she can carry. She's too proud, though, living in a crappy apartment downtown, driving around in a car that looks like it's on its last leg. I mean, shit, I'm glad she's not walking around anymore, and I was this close to just leaving one outside her door, but that's because I'm not smooth. Not like Nicholas. Not subtle, either.

I'm a predator who can be silent when he has to, but with little impulse control.

That's why I did my best to stay away. Because if I didn't? Stalking is one thing. So are my annual kills. But there was a good chance I'd add kidnapping to my list of crimes, and my twin was right: I will never, ever fucking hurt this woman.

But I'm sure as hell going to make her feel good tonight…

"Wait… does that mean I get four thousand dollars if I can escape you? By when?"

Holy shit. Two thousand is nothing to Nicholas, but I've never seen him pay that much for me.

He must have really wanted to give me Sally for our birthday. And, shit, I really want to have her.

Four grand? It's a bargain. For one chance to fuck her the way I've spent months fantasizing over… there isn't a price I wouldn't pay.

She'll learn that in time. For now, on a spark of

perverted genius, I tell her, "By midnight tomorrow. At the end of Halloween. But it has to be Halloween night. You leave me before dawn, it's just the two grand."

I'll follow the first two rules—but now that she's here… can I bring myself to follow the third?

We'll find out, won't we?

Sally nibbles her bottom lip again. It's adorable. "That's twenty-four hours."

"Isn't that what you promised me?"

"Well—I *guess*. But I thought…"

I can only imagine what she thought.

Probably not that I planned on chasing her over five acres, or that any fucking that we do will be out here. With the big house at my back, she must've thought I'd invite her in there—and on any other night, I might've. I never have before, but this is Sally… and as much as that changes most things, it doesn't change *everything*.

I reach into my pocket, pulling out a single metal key, passing it off to her.

"Don't lose this."

It hits her a moment later that she doesn't have anything on her: no pockets, no phone, no purse. My twin would've told her not to bring anything she didn't want to lose, and she listened.

Now she has my key and, after a second, she slips it inside the cup of her bra.

I nod at her. "There's a cabin on the property. It's

about an acre or so away from the house, just past the part of the cemetery where all of the Reeds are buried. You can't miss it. If you're still here when the sun comes up, go to the cabin. Let yourself in. Rest. And then I'll see you again when the sun goes down and it's dark."

Was she listening to me? Almost at once, she turns around, looking at the graves beyond the iron-wrought fence that fills up our entire backyard, stretching out as far as the eye can see.

"Aren't those all Reeds?" she asks.

Smart girl. Observant.

"No."

She licks her lips, then swallows roughly. I follow the motion of her throat with my gaze, glad the skeleton mask hides just how much I want to lift it up to my nose, then trace the column on her pale white skin with my tongue.

Fear is intoxicating to me. Her apprehension… a fucking aphrodisiac. And the way she's trembling— not because of the late October chill anymore, but because reality is sinking in—has my cock desperate to find its home inside of my sweet Sally.

Not yet.

"But don't you worry about that. Tonight… this is just me and you. Remember, if I find you… if I *catch* you… I'm gonna fuck you. And you want me to, don't you?"

I don't know what I would've done if she had

come to her senses and realized that this was too much for her. Would I have let her go? Or would I have chased after her anyway?

It doesn't matter. Because Sally… my innocent little doe takes a deep breath, then nods.

"*Yes.*"

Thank fucking God.

I reach for my holster with one hand. With the other, I crook my finger, gesturing for her to come closer.

She doesn't even hesitate.

I grab the handle of my knife. The blade frees itself easily, the moonlight reflecting off of the steel as it slides out of the holster. It won't be pristine for long —it never is on Halloween—but the gleam draws her attention to my favorite weapon.

She shudders.

It's fucking *delicious*.

Laying my hand on her hip, I give her a squeeze, then drag her the rest of the way toward me. I'm already as hard as I can possibly be but I can tell that sweet Sally, my precious with her big doe eyes, is hovering on the edge. If I push her too much, too fast, she'll fall and I'll break her instead of bending her, shaping her, turning her into *mine*.

Because she is. She has been from the moment she crossed my path.

And I'm done with pretending she isn't.

When we're so close that we're breathing the same

air even through the fabric of my mask, I drop to my knees in front of her. With my knife in one hand, I use the other to hike up her skirt.

Forget breathing the same air. This close, I get my first whiff of her fresh pussy through the tiny bit of fabric covering her mound.

The thong makes it easy for me to do what I want to do. Two quick slices, one on each side of her, and her panties are only being held up by the way her thighs are clenched tightly together.

I tug, removing them completely.

"Hunter," she gasps. "What—"

"Making it easy for later," I tell her. "Because, trust me, you won't have any need for these."

Rising up, I pocket the scraps of fabric. Then, sliding the knife back into its holster, I tell her honestly, "Now run, sweet Sally, run… because if you can't escape me, you're mine… forever."

Does she know I'm dead fucking serious? For a moment there, I don't think so. She gapes at me, but if it's because of what I said or because I just cut her panties off of her, I can't tell.

Probably both.

"Hunter—"

"Five."

"Hunter, you… let's go inside. We can talk about this."

Nope. "Four."

"I… I know what I agreed to. But it's dark out there."

"And it's safe. Look. You see that? There's a fence surrounding our backyard cemetery that's higher than you and me both that no one can climb. Nothing will hurt you. The opposite, in fact. When I find you… three."

Dipping her hand beneath her bra, she shows me the key I gave her. "What if I find the cabin?"

It's better than her finding the single gap in the fence that she could escape once she crosses onto the cemetery. "Go right ahead. It's yours tonight." And, once I call Nicholas, giving him some updated instructions now that I know who my gift is, it'll be perfect for her. "Two."

I never get to 'one'. Before I do, Sally squeals and, without a look back at me, she runs through the wide opening in the fence that leads her away from the house and into the Reed family graveyard.

I wait a few moments to give her a head start. It's more fun this way, and I want to really enjoy this chase.

Then, once I don't see a flash of white in the distance, I stalk through the gates myself. Grabbing one of the open doors, I shove it closed. I do the same for the other. There's a lock hanging loose on one side. With a quick snap, it's shut, blocking off this exit.

Now, if Sally does want to leave me, she'll have only the one path out.

I chuckle into the darkness. Good luck finding it…

Whistling under my breath, in a much better mood than I've been in for weeks, I start to stroll into the graveyard myself, pausing once only to call out, "Come out, come out, little doe," so that she knows I'm already behind her.

And if I'm as good of a tracker as I think I am, I'll be on her—and inside of her—before she knows it.

Yes.

COME OUT, COME OUT,
little doe...

12:43 AM

SALLY

"**C**ome out, come out, little doe."

The sing-songy lilt to his alluring voice shouldn't affect me as much as it does. Especially since there's something about it being a masked man saying it, cutting through the quiet of the night.

I have my hands clapped over my mouth as I run as quickly yet as *quietly* as I can. I'm afraid he'll hear me whimper and know exactly where to find me.

And then… and then he'll have me.

Now, I came out to this huge house, knowing that I was going to have sex with Hunter. He made that very clear when he invited me up here, and once I accepted the promise of the two grand from him, this became sex work. It's not something I haven't thought about doing before, especially after what happened with Max, and at least I know my first customer.

If that *is* my first customer…

The mask threw me. When Hunter's boots hit the back porch, his big body looking even bigger outside of his usual suits, my immediate instinct was to bolt. Something about him was off. Different. He wasn't the Hunter Reed I've gotten to know over these last four months even if he sounded like him.

Then he started laying out the rules, never once explaining why he has his face covered, and there was never a chance for me to really ask.

Same thing with this dress I've got on.

It's cold out. I thought it would be when I first saw the dress out of its box, but it's even chillier than I expected. Probably because it's after midnight and it's just more of a slip than anything else, but still.

I was freezing before. Now, I'm too scared shitless to even notice the weather.

I'm in a graveyard. Marble slabs, headstones of all shapes and sizes—most of them unmarked—and even some large stone angels dot the spooky land. There are trees everywhere. Bushes, too. Maybe it's well landscaped in the afternoon, but at midnight?

I feel like a heroine straight out of a horror movie.

It's not just my surroundings, either. I'm in a tiny dress that could double as a nightgown, tottering on heels that were meant to make me look sexy but are killer to run in, and I have a masked man with a knife chasing after me.

Sure, he used the knife to slice off my thong before pocketing it, and he's chasing me with the intention of fucking me on Halloween… but this isn't what I expected.

Well, the sex part, yes. But that was all.

I came prepared. I have a plan B in my purse in case Hunter doesn't want to bother with protection during his game. Before I agreed to this madness, I did insist on seeing his test results so that I knew he was clean. His were from three months ago and he swore on his father's grave that he'd been too busy to be intimate with anyone since then.

He runs the two largest businesses in Shadowvale. For all I know he might have been.

As for me, I sure as hell got my results after I found out Max cheated on me. I mean, I was in the hospital anyway and it just made sense. I offered to show them to Hunter on my phone and he read them quickly, then repeated his invitation to me.

So, yes, sex was always going to happen. I just… when he said he liked to play games, I didn't think it entailed me running in heels during the most adult version of hide and seek I've ever seen.

I can't just let him catch me. I promised to play the game, and something tells me that he'll consider it cheating if I don't at least *try* to get away.

This is his family's home. I can't outrun him, and

if I keep running anyway, he'll use some kind of shortcut to track me down. My best bet is to hide.

When I see a large headstone tucked in the middle of a closely-grown copse of naked trees, I drop down behind it and hope that he can't spot my bright white dress from a distance.

I don't know how long I'm hiding for. After the first time I heard him sing out, using a nickname for me I've only hear him use once before, he went silent —and I mean *silent*. His heavy footfall is swallowed up by the quiet to the point that all I hear is the thud of my pulse and my quickened breath.

I don't have my phone. Except for the key jabbing into my boob, I don't have *anything*. I left all of my belongings back in my car like Hunter told me to.

It seems like an eternity, though I'm not sure it's really been that long when, all of a sudden, he steps out from behind the nearest tree.

"There you are. I found you."

I start to hop to my feet, ready to run again, but Hunter is too fast. He's there before I'm halfway off the ground, grabbing me in a bear hug.

"What are you—"

"Tut, tut, little doe. Don't you remember what you agreed to? If I catch you, I get to do what I want."

I know. And I instantly interpreted that to mean we would fuck as soon as he tracked me down. I thought I was prepared for it, too, but when he keeps my hands pinned at my sides, all but dragging me in front of the headstone I was crouching behind, I'm beginning to have second thoughts.

They become third thoughts when places me right in the center of it, using his palm to guide me down so that I'm bending over it.

I couldn't have picked a worse one to hide behind if I tried. It's freaking huge so it's hip-height—which means it's just the right size for him to bend me over and have access to my bare pussy with only bending his knees if he wants to take me like this.

The chill of the grave marker cuts through the thin material of my dress, but when I shiver, it's with an anticipation that goes from my damp pussy all the way to my tender toes.

"Brace your elbows," he commands. "Grab whatever part of the stone you want, but get ready. When you squirm, I don't want you getting hurt."

Because he promised I wouldn't.

But squirm? Why does he think I'm going to squirm?

I get the answer to that almost immediately when his big hand plants against the middle of my back, pushing me down so that I'm completely bent over the headstone. Like he told me to, I lock my elbows and brace my forearms against the smooth rock, arching my back as he flips my skirt up, baring my ass to him.

Smack!

"You like that, little doe?" Before I can answer, the

flat of his palm finds my stinging cheek again. I gasp, and he chuckles lowly. "You naughty girl. You can take a little pain, can't you? But only when it's followed by pleasure."

I hate pain. I hate being hurt. I had enough of that with Max, but there's a difference between what Hunter just did and my ex's slaps. Hunter spanked me, trying to make me feel good. Max… he would slap me around, hoping it hurt.

"I'd rather have pleasure," I say at last, swallowing a moan.

"Just what I wanted to hear, sweet Sally. I've been dying for a taste."

Something about the way he rumbles that has me looking over my shoulder at Hunter.

The cloth mask with the skeleton print on it covers his entire head. There's gotta be a way for him to see through it, but he said 'taste'.

How is he supposed to do that while wearing a full face covering? Is that really what he means by 'taste'? And, yeah, I did agree to do whatever it was that he wanted me to… but is he really going to choose to go down on *me* instead?

"What's the matter, baby? What's on your mind?"

A hundred things, including—

"I just… how are you going to do that with the mask on?"

In answer, he reaches for his knife. Pulling it out, he lifts the point to his face. One quick slash and he's created a slit in the fabric. Once the knife's away, he sticks out his tongue, wagging it at me.

I blink.

He chuckles. "When there's a will, there's a way."

You can say that again.

"And you're sure… I mean, you're really are Hunter under there?"

I don't mean for my question to come out as doubting as it did. I'm the woman this masked man picked for his Halloween fun, and I'm here. I came. I'm not some innocent little virgin who had no clue what she signed up for.

But that's the thing. I signed up to spend this night with Hunter Reed.

This guy sounds like Hunter. He's about the same size, too. I *think* it's him… but I don't know. With that mask on, he could be *anyone*.

He rests his hands on my waist, lifting me so that I'm standing again instead of being bent over the big slab of marble.

Hunter gestures for me to turn completely, to face him head-on.

I do.

Bracing his boots in the grass, he crosses his arms over his chest. His voice is full of some kind of sly humor as he says, "Go on. Ask me something only he'll know. Let me prove I'm Hunter Reed."

I can do that. In fact, I'm so grateful he's giving me this chance. I'll let him do whatever he wants to me—but I'd feel a lot better if I knew it really was Hunter under that mask.

"What's your birthday?"

"Halloween."

Wait—*today*?

"Seriously?"

At his nod, I tell him, "Oh. I guess I didn't know that. Well, um, happy birthday."

"Thanks. Now try again."

Okay. "You have a brother. What's his name?"

He shakes his head, like he expects better from me. "Nicholas. Still too easy, Sally. Try again."

What's something that Hunter would know?

"Alright. You helped me get my car. What year is it, and what color?"

"Now you've got the hang of things." He chuckles. "Your car is an '03. Teal green, your favorite color."

Hm. If he saw me pull up and went to see my car, he might know that.

"One more," I say. "Your coffee order. What is it?"

"I'm not a big coffee drinker, but when I do, I take it black with a little bit of cream." He pauses for a moment, cocking his head slightly. "I *like* cream."

My cheeks heat up at his obvious double meaning.

Ignoring that, I say, "Not a coffee drinker? I see you almost every day."

"Right. I'm not a fan of coffee, but I am a fan of you."

Oh.

He's flirting with me the same way Hunter does. He knows about my car, and how he takes his coffee.

It has to be him.

I give him a shy smile. Ironic since he has my panties in his pocket and I'm wet as hell at the promise of what's to come, but my voice is soft as I admit, "I like you, too, Hunter."

Should I? Maybe not, but that's not gonna stop me, is it?

"Glad to hear it, little doe. You ready to do this now?"

"I guess so."

Hunter huffs. "No guessing here. Before I touch you again, I have to make sure you're all in. For the money, because you've been thinking about fucking me while making those silly espresso drinks… because I'm here and you're wet and it's probably been ages since you had a man fuck you with his tongue. It doesn't matter why you're here, just that no one's forcing you to be here. Understand?"

I bob my head. "Yes."

"Then bend over again."

I do. Assuming the same position as before, I bend over the headstone myself.

Another slap on my bare ass after he flips up my

skirt. I swallow another moan, anticipating what he's going to do next.

"Don't turn around," he orders. "You made a good point before. When I get my mouth on you, I'm not just using my tongue. I'm gonna get all up in there, baby, and the mask might get in my way. I'm gonna hike it up a little so keep your head down."

I listen, even as I ask, "And you're sure I can't see you?"

"Where is the fun in that, little doe?"

I want to ask him about that name. Where did it come from? Why does he keep using it on me? But, before I get the chance, he hits the dirt with his knees. Big, warm hands grip my ass cheeks, spreading me wide as he does exactly what he said he would do.

Hunter eats me out from behind.

He starts near my clit, sucking it and one of my labia right into his mouth. His tongue swirls around my clit, teeth bumping up against the engorged button before he uses the flat of his tongue to taste me from clit all the way up to my opening.

"God, that's fucking good," he says, rumbling against my pussy before he nuzzles the whole damn thing.

I can feel his skin against mine, hear the moisture slicking against it, the rustle of the fabric on his mask from where he has it yanked up over his nose.

He licks again, gathering up all the cream he implied he liked, groaning as he swallows.

Then, right as I'm pushing back against him, trapped between his face and the headstone, he curls his tongue and dips it inside of me.

I pant, and Hunter squeezes my ass cheek even as he keeps on fucking me with his tongue.

Digging my nails into the backside of the rough marble, I'm sure I'm losing all the layers of skin on my fingertips beneath it but I just don't give a fuck. His warm mouth feels so good on me. When he releases my ass cheek, sliding his thumb to play with the pucker of my asshole, I clench, then grunt when I get another slap for my trouble.

Pulling away, he presses his teeth against my stinging cheek. He doesn't bite, not really, but it's an obvious warning.

"What I want, little doe. I get what I want. If that means my tongue in your cunt or my finger up your ass, you take it like my good girl. You hear me?"

I nod.

He bites a little harder and, *fuck*, that should not have been enough to bring me to the brink of coming all over his face—but it does, and the way my lower body convulses lets him know that.

Releasing my skin, he rubs my ass, then moves his hand to my clitoral hood. Dipping his fingers beneath it, he tweaks my clit between two of them.

That does it. Right as he returns his face to my pussy, I lose complete control and start coming.

Once I'm done, once I have to whimper and beg

and plead for me to finally give me a little relief, the only thing I remember as I slump over the headstone is Hunter's self-satisfied chuckle as he rumbles, "I knew you'd be fucking sweet."

And I knew, from the moment I met Hunter Reed, that no one would make me come harder than anyone else had before him.

Looks like we were both right.

COME OUT, COME OUT,
little doe...

HUNTER

It's one hour into Halloween, and Sally's pussy is the sweetest candy I've ever fucking tasted.

I should have given her a little bit more time to recover, but that's what happens when you're an addict who falls off the wagon just the once. It's so easy to take another hit, take another bump, take another shot after that first one.

I had a taste of her—and I need *more*.

Before, she avoided me for nearly forty minutes. I admit, I allowed her to stay one step ahead of me because I get nearly as much pleasure out of stalking my prey as I do touching them or having them touch me.

Normally, the first time I catch one of my girls, the darkness inside of me needs to see them on their knees. At that moment, I am their God, and fuck if my cock doesn't need to be worshiped.

But with Sally… I could've told her to open her mouth, slipping my cock between her lips. The look on her face told me that was what she expected *and* what she wanted.

Sorry to disappoint, little doe, but I found you. That meant I got to do what I wanted, and as much as I enjoy a good blowjob like any other hot-blooded guy, I needed to conquer my Sally. I needed her at my mercy, panting softly, keening with pleasure that *I* gave her.

I needed to show her that she could trust me when I told her that I would never hurt her. A little pain might work to get me off, but Sally… she's different. With her, until I can see how far I can push her, I'll let her get used to me.

And after my first lick up her slit, I know I'm already dying for another taste.

I'm addicted. My goal tonight is to earn what I can, eventually take what I can't, and make her just as addicted to me.

I've done it before. Not on purpose, though. Some of my girls liked what I did for them—whether it was the mask that did it, the chase, or the way I worked my cock—and were desperate for more.

But that's not my style. Before Sally, I was a one-and-done; another reason why I knew I shouldn't fuck with her. The more I tried to forget her, the more I had to tell myself that it was pointless. If I got my hands on her, I'd never want to let her go.

And I learned that already when I had her bent over some nameless grave, devouring her delicious pussy.

When I run her down again a few minutes after I let her go, I sneak around the darkness, using the shadows to hide me until I cut her off. She runs right into my waiting arms, moving so quickly through the scattered graves that she didn't notice me until I moved out from behind a massive carved stone angel.

Her tits press against my chest, her hands instinctively going to my waist as though part of her already understands that she can trust me.

A short shriek escapes her. It's one of surprise, and she strangles it when she sees my mask and gasps, "Hunter? Tell me that's you."

"I told you before, little doe. There's no one else out here except you and me."

"I know. Sorry." She giggles nervously. "It's the mask. I just keep thinking there might be someone else under there. Someone I don't know."

She lets go of my waist.

I immediately drop my hands on hers.

Lifting her up, I grin beneath the mask as she squeals again. I ignore the sound, even though my throbbing cock doesn't.

"It's Halloween," is all I say. "What final girl

doesn't want to be chased by a man in a mask, then fucked by him?"

"Is that… is that what's going to happen now?"

She's so breathless, so immediately *aroused*, that I almost say 'fuck it' and throw her to the grass. I know exactly what I'll find beneath her dress, and I'm dying for it.

It takes all the self-control I didn't know I had to follow through with my initial plan. Hefting her higher, showing her that—despite my size and strength—I can be gentle with her, I set her down on the nearest flat headstone that I see.

The moment I do, she yelps.

"What's the matter?"

"My ass is cold," she admits sheepishly.

"Good. Maybe you need to cool off a little right now."

Sally frowns, though her expression changes when I take one of her muddy bare feet in my hand.

"Where are your heels, Sally?"

Her breath catches in her throat as I stroke the sole of her foot, then her ankle. "I… I kicked them off. Made running easier."

That's what I figured.

"Just be careful that you don't trip. I don't want to see you hurt, not even for our little game."

"I won't."

"Good."

I follow the curve of her calf, reaching up her thigh.

She whimpers as I shift my hand, stroking the inner part.

I'm inches away from her heat and already I can tell that she's too worked up for me to tease.

I'm going to do it anyway, though.

Addicted, I think. I'm a lost fucking cause already, but I need her to want me even a fraction that I do her.

I'm not above using pleasure to control her. Not tonight.

Not on Halloween.

I lay my left hand on her hip, pinning her in place right before I slip the pointer finger on my other hand past her pussy lips, tracing her slit.

"You're even wetter than before."

She doesn't even say a real word. That sound she makes is more like a mewling plea that only assures me what I knew from the moment I laid eyes on her: this woman is *mine*.

"Do you want me to fuck you?"

"Hunter—"

"I said, do you want me to fuck you, Sally?"

"I… *yes*."

I want that, too. I want that more than anything.

And that's precisely why I slip my hand out from under her dress again.

She blinks, almost like she thinks I'm rejecting her, and fuck no… we can't have that, can we?

From the moment Nicholas gave me her, I think I was already planning on keeping Sally. Every minute I spend with her instead of watching her from a distance, torturing myself for no reason than the pain reminds me I'm alive—and because even I know she's too good for me—is another minute that I realize this was inevitable.

For four months, I stayed away. I fucked my fist, fantasizing it was her sweet pussy, and on more than one occasion I marked the final stair on her fire escape with my come as though I was an animal marking its territory.

But now… I don't have to stay away, do I?

I take her by the chin, tilting her head back so that she has no choice but to look up at my masked face.

She can't see me, but she instinctively knows that she's mine. As I gaze down into her doe eyes, I see hunger and lust, and a desperate need that calls to the depravity inside of me.

Jerking up the bottom part of the mask, freeing only my lips, I slam mine down on hers.

She gasps, then groans, opening her mouth to let me inside.

Does she taste herself on me? That thought has me grinding my erection on the headstone that I have Sally still perched on. It's only fair. The chilly stone is freezing her ass, while the rough rock is managing to scratch my sensitive skin through my jeans.

I'm torturing both of us now—and I like it.

We're both breathing heavier than before when I break the kiss. Pausing only to yank my mask back down, I run my thumb along the side of her jaw.

"If I catch you, I get what I want. Maybe you should catch *me*, little doe."

I could fuck her right now. She would let me, but I want my first time working my way into her cunt to mean something to both of us.

She thinks she knows Hunter Reed. She met the side that Nicholas knows how to show off, but not even my twin can tap into the true depravity that comes with being the younger Reed.

He keeps his darkness hidden behind closed doors, only losing control when he's in his red room.

Me? I don it like a mask, only removing it when I fucking feel like it.

Sally thinks she can handle me. Can handle what's existed between us since the moment I caught sight of her, tempting me as she strolled down that back street, oblivious to all of the dangers in this world.

Maybe she can.

But the rules of this game have just changed—and I think we both know *that*.

COME OUT, COME OUT,
little doe…

SIX

OCTOBER 31ST

2:38 AM

SALLY

He switched the game on me.

It's still hide and seek, but now? I'm the one who's 'it', I guess.

Wait… that's tag, isn't it?

Doesn't matter. Hunter dared me to find him, and if there's one thing he's learned about me through our daily encounters at the café, it's this: I can't turn down a dare.

Later, I'll ask myself if that's the only reason I started searching for him. It's not like I didn't know what would happen if I managed to find him, or that I honestly believed that if I *couldn't* Hunter wouldn't just turn around and proclaim cockily that he found *me* a third time.

I won't see the sun again without having that man

inside of me. I think we both know that. It's just a matter of if he lets me find him so that he can have the pleasure of hearing me ask for it, or if he stops ignoring the erection I felt earlier and uses it.

He's right. I would've fucked him on that grave marker without a doubt, and when he found me the second time, checking to see how wet he makes me, I would've begged for him to shuck his pants if I thought it would work.

It won't. Because if there's something I've learned about *Hunter*, it's that he's going to play his game the way he wants. Besides, what's the rush? I have until midnight tomorrow night to let him chase me the way he wants to, mask and all.

He wants me to find him. When I hear a twig crackling in the distance, immediately darting off in that direction, I wonder if this is a trap. The same thing occurs to me when I hear a husky chuckle, then a whisper, aware that he's luring me closer but not doing a damn thing about it.

But when I stumble over a root I didn't see in the dark, nearly face-planting before a pair of strong arms come out of nowhere to catch me, I have to admit that he herded me right where he wanted me.

It worked, too. I found him—and when I see why he caught me, humming under his breath before he tells me, "Not so close, Sally," I nearly turn on my heel and dash off into the woods again.

There's a hole in the middle of his family's property. A big ass hole, shaped like a narrow rectangle, at least six feet deep.

Six feet deep…

Holy fucking shit.

That's not just a hole.

It's a *grave*.

"Let me down," I say, much calmer than I feel.

"You caught me. Is that what you want?"

"Just… please. Put me down."

Okay. I wasn't so calm that time.

Hearing the hysteria creeping its way into my voice, Hunter nuzzles his mask against my temple before swinging me around, setting me on my feet with enough space between me and the grave that I won't risk tripping again and falling into it.

As soon as I'm standing again, the scratchy grass tickling between my dirt-covered toes, I edge toward the grave. Peeking down, using the moonlight to help me, I notice that there's a blanket spread out down there. A deep red, if I'm not wrong, but definitely a fleece blanket.

Why is there a blanket covering the dirt?

Oh God.

Oh my *God*.

He… this is it, isn't it? He made me bend over a grave marker so that he could go down on me, and after he teased me on another one so that I nearly *begged* for him to fuck me, he found a way to lead me here so that he could—and he plans on doing so in a freshly dug grave.

Because that's what it is. On the other side of the hole, I see a mound of dirt and a fucking *shovel*. It's a grave, with a blanket, and when I turn around to gape at him, all I get is the skeleton's mocking grin staring back at me.

What was I thinking? As much as I wanted to prove that I could handle Hunter Reed, I'm beginning to understand that there's a reason why everyone in Shadowvale says to stay away from him.

He's not just dangerous. He's a fucking *psycho*.

Before I can disappear into the woods, his hands land on both of my upper arms.

His grip is tight, but he's still careful not to hurt me as he presses his fingers into my flesh before he lifts me up off of the slick grass, yanking me backward so that my back slams against his hard chest and even harder cock.

Setting me down on the ground again, he pushes his hips out, making sure I can't miss the bulge in his jeans as he shoves his erection into the small of my back.

"Why are you running, Sally? You caught me. That means you can tell me what you want to do… but if you run and I grab you… and I *will* grab you, baby… then it's on me."

Why is he pretending? No matter what, I'm not getting out of here without him fucking me, and even if I avoid the grave now, will I be able to avoid it before I can escape?

Probably not, but I have to ask him. I have to make him hear it so that he understands just how crazy this is.

"And what then? You catch me, I play your game by the rules, and you fuck me in a *grave*?"

His breath is warm on my skin as he chuckles behind me. "If it makes you feel any better, it's not yours."

Strangely enough, that *doesn't*.

"Whose is it?"

"Don't you worry about that. That's my business. My brother's, too. Not yours, sweet Sally. At least, not now."

I shake my head. "I don't like this. I… I think I should go."

"You could. All of this only happens if you want it to. But, please…" He moves his hips, pushing that bulge up against my ass. "Don't lie to me. Don't lie to yourself, either. You want this as bad as I do. Bad enough that if I tell you to climb down there, you will, so long as I promise to let you out again."

"I— *no*. It's a grave!"

"Not yet it isn't. It needs a corpse to be a grave, and you and me…" He rolls his hips again. "We're very much alive. Don't let the skeleton mask fool you. I'm not dead. You won't be. But wouldn't you rather enjoy the ride out of the elements?" Another chuckle. "I put a blanket down there for cushion."

I'm not kidding. This guy is fucking *nuts*.

But I might just be, too, because he's actually managing to talk me into this.

I have one condition, though.

"I found you, right? That's what you said? You want me to go in that hole? Fine. But I want something first."

He tilts his head. I don't think he expected it would be that easy to convince me. I'm surprised a bit myself. This whole thing is insane… and, yet, this is Hunter Reed. I haven't been able to forget him for months, and maybe this is what I need to do to do just that.

"Anything for you, little doe."

"Take off the mask."

I expect him to say, "Anything but that."

I'm pushing my luck. I know I am. He made it clear from the beginning that the mask stays on and the panties come off. And I was okay with that when he was chasing after me. Now that I'm actually about to be more vulnerable than I have been… now that I'm about to let him shove his cock inside of me, I need to see his face.

This is Hunter. He satisfied my doubts with his answers earlier, but that's not why I need to see him. Even when I have a one-night stand, I have to be able to look in their eyes.

I'm prepared to explain myself, but I don't have to. After a moment's pause where I bet he's weighing the odds of me going through with this if he refuses, he nods.

"You caught me," is all he says before he grips his mask by the bottom, yanking it up and over his head.

His normally styled hair is flat against his skull from all the time he wore the mask. He runs his fingers through it before tossing the mask to the dirt, a familiar grin quirking his lips as he looks down at me.

"There. Hunter Reed in the flesh. Happy, baby?"

I might be—if this was Hunter Reed.

It's not.

That's not Hunter.

I don't even know what it is about him that's wrong. His eyes are the same shade of blue. His features are the same. His hair is messy, but if it was combed, it would be the fucking same.

But this isn't Hunter.

I take a step back from him. Another. Throwing up my hands, shaking my head slowly, I stare at him anyway, trying to figure out what it is that has my senses pinging like mad.

It finally hits me. There. His cheek. The right one. The Hunter I know… the Hunter I've gazed at, dreamed about, obsessed over… he has a small beauty mark on his right cheek.

This guy *doesn't*.

"Who are you?"

"Sally, be careful. You don't want to fall in that pit."

Fuck the pit. "Who *are* you?"

"I told you. I'm Hunter Reed."

"Bullshit," I snap. "The Hunter I know has a beauty mark. Unless you lasered it off since yesterday or… or you got make-up on for Halloween or something, you're not Hunter."

Even if he is wearing make-up, that wouldn't explain it. Seeing his face, I just *know* that he isn't *my* Hunter.

And then he says, "Oh. You must be talking about Nicholas."

What? "He… you… he said his name was Hunter. I've been talking to Hunter for months now. Making him coffee, trying to catch his… your… attention. He invited me here to play this game. He *said* he was *Hunter*."

"Right." His tone is low. Soothing. "Because he was. Now I am."

I was right. He's insane. Or maybe he has multiple personalities, one of them named after his older brother. Because Nicholas is his brother, but not Hunter and, holy shit, I think I might throw up.

"He said he was Hunter," I repeat.

"I know, baby. And, like I said, he was."

Before I can actually throw up, Hunter— "Hunter"—pulls his phone out of his back pocket.

After fiddling with it for a moment, he turns the screen around.

The same man is pictured twice: one in a suit, the other in a henley shirt and jeans. They have their arms slung around each other, duplicates, but when I peer closer, I see that one of them has a beauty mark on his cheek—and the other one doesn't.

He might be crazy, I realize, glancing up at him again, but he also is a *twin*.

"What? *Why*?"

"He knew how much I wanted you," he confesses, slipping his phone back into his pocket. "How there wouldn't be any gift better than my little doe running around our property, letting me chase her for real instead of watching her from the shadows… so he was Hunter, but now that you're here, I am."

My mind is blown.

Four months. I've lived in Shadowvale for more than four months. Everything I heard said that Nicholas Reed was the older Reed brother.

Why did no one ever mention that they were fucking *twins*?

"I *am* Hunter," he says, inching toward me, trying to keep me from spooking and running after all. "I'm the man who would do anything for you. The man who will give you everything… if only you'll let me have this."

Reaching out slowly, he doesn't stop until his hand is on my shoulder.

When I don't immediately shake him off, he slides it down, cupping my elbow before dropping his palm to my hip.

I still don't move away from him. In fact, I actually move closer to him because… I honestly don't even know why except that he's intoxicating and I'm a fucking idiot.

He takes heart in how close we are. His blue eyes seem to gleam with promise as he squeezes my hip, then continues traveling, his fingers searching until they find my pussy through the silk material of my dress.

I gasp.

Hunter grins.

"Did my brother touch you? When he was me, did you let him do this?"

Slowly, surely, *possessively,* he fingers me through the material.

"No," I say, my breath shaky. I shift my lower half, trying to entice him to dip his fingers inside of me. Suddenly, I'm achy and I'm empty, and I couldn't care less who he is so long as he keeps touching me like this.

"What about this?" He bends his head, brushing his lips against mine. "Did he kiss you?"

"Never. Actually, I don't think he ever touched me at all."

Anytime he made a move to do so, he was careful

to keep a small buffer between us. I thought he was being respectful—and maybe he was.

Not of me, though, but his twin.

Hunter confirms that.

"We have a line. Maybe we shouldn't bother, considering everything else we do, but we don't share. We don't poach, either. If I want you, you're Hunter's no matter which twin you're with. But if he touched you…"

His hand moves away from me to my utter disappointment, but when I see that he's traded my pussy for his knife, I go completely still.

He likes that reaction even more.

Hunter shows me the knife, then places the point to the crook of my elbow. I don't know what he planned on doing until, suddenly, it hurts and he's waiting to see how I'll react next.

I smack him in the chest with my free hand. "What was that?"

"Did it hurt? More than you can handle?"

He has no idea how high my tolerance is. I don't like it, but I can handle it, and I tell him that. "I'm fine. I just don't know why you did that."

"Don't you?"

The knife disappears now that it's done its job. Dipping his finger into the crook of my elbow, he makes sure I can see that the tip is coated with enough blood for it to be noticeable.

He must've cut me deeper than I first thought,

and I still have no clue why… and then he pops his finger into his mouth, laving the digit clean.

"You're inside of me," he drawls once he's done. "And now? I'm about to be inside of you."

Hunter looks at me with a dare written in every line of his handsome face. For a moment, he steps aside, showing me a path I could take to get away from him.

When I stay right where I am, he takes that as the silent consent I mean it as. And then, before I know it, he's getting undressed and there isn't a bone in my body that wants to walk away from him now.

As I'm watching, he tugs on the zipper, shoving his jeans so that they're under his ass. His cock—already so swollen with need, it's got a bead of pre-come at the tip, begging me to taste—springs out, bobbing its way toward me.

I swipe my thumb over it, gathering the moisture. Then, meeting his gaze, I lick it.

"Does that count?"

"Oh, baby, you can take that drop now, but by the time I'm done with you, your pussy will be full of it."

He's not boasting, either. It's a promise.

His cock out, Hunter crouches low, easing himself into the hole. He looks up at me, waiting expectantly.

I could run. It would take him a minute to jump back out and zip up, giving me a head start.

I *could* run—but I don't.

Instead, I hold my breath and do something I never thought I would: jump willingly into a grave.

Hunter is there to catch me. At least, that's what I *thought* he was doing. I should've known better. The second he has me steady, he pulls me closer, his lips hot on my ear as he tells me, "Get on all fours."

It's the command in his tone that doesn't even have me questioning him. He wants me on all fours? I drop down on all fours.

The blanket is fleece, I confirm. It's soft and warm, and—damn it—Hunter's right. We're out of the elements down here, without the wind whipping past us. I'm already warmer than I have been, but then Hunter covers my back with his big body and I'm fucking *hot*.

"Next time, I'm looking you in your eyes when I make you mine. They're fucking gorgeous, but after you let me feast on your pussy while gazing at your ass? I've been thinking about taking you from behind all night, little doe. After all, tonight? We're both animals. Why not rut?"

If that's what he wants to call it.

He's not wrong. The chase… the run… the teasing… it's all led up to this moment. It kinda feels right, arching my back, sticking my ass in the air, enticing him as I wait for the moment he lodges the head of his cock inside of me and pushes.

And when he does? I throw back my head, letting

the howl rip out of my throat, almost like I'm a damn werewolf on Halloween.

I knew he was big from that one glimpse I got of him. In this position, he's even more massive, and if he hasn't spent the first part of this night playing with me, getting me ready with his tongue and his fingers before, I don't know if I could take him as easily as I am.

But when he bows over me, the skirt of my dress trapped between me and him, his teeth finding my bare shoulder, I'm ready to take all he has to offer.

He starts slow, as though afraid he'll spill right away. Reaching around me, he palms my tit through the dress, squeezing it, caressing it.

"You doing okay, Sally?"

I nod. I'm so full, stretched to my limits with him hitting every single one of my nerves as he goes in, then out, that I can't even find the words to tell him just how 'okay' I'm doing right now.

"You're such a good girl. Taking me like this, letting me do whatever the fuck I want to you with nothing but a whimper and a moan... I knew you were the one. From the moment our eyes met... you understand me, don't you?"

Honestly? I wish I did.

"You're not afraid." That part, at least, is true. "You've never been afraid. Not of my rep. Not of my family's rep. Not even of my mask... that turned you on, baby, didn't it?"

I arch up into him, swallowing my cry of pleasure as I gasp out, "Yes."

"What about this? What about knowing you're fucking the man who watched you, not the one who pretended he did?"

I still don't understand what that means.

But I do know *one* thing.

"I just want you, Hunter. Unh… that's all… that's all I ever wanted."

He pulls out, slamming into me, making my whole body nearly collapse from the sheer pleasure of it all. "And you have him. So take him, little doe, and know that this is just the beginning."

That's right. Because we have the rest of tonight, and tomorrow.

Unless I escape, that is—

"*Sally*. My sweet, sweet, Sally…"

—yeah… I'm not trying to get away from this man anytime soon, am I?

***

LONG AFTER HUNTER CLIMBS OFF OF ME, ZIPPING HIS jeans back up and redoing his belt buckle, my legs are still too shaky to hold my weight.

He wrecked me. There's no other word for how thoroughly he possessed my body the way he did, touching parts of me that none of my previous lovers ever had before. And not just the way he angled my back so that he could stroke deeper, bottoming out inside of me in order to come.

It's the way he checked in with me the entire time. Sex was inevitable, but I was an active partner the whole time. It wasn't like Max, who treated me like a replaceable sex doll on his good days. He made sure to put my pleasure first, caressing my boobs, rubbing my back, and reaching around us to pay special attention to my clit when it became obvious that I'm not the kind of chick who comes from penetration alone. I need a little more stimulation than that, and as though making up for that little nick he gave me with his knife, he put all of my pleasure first before taking his own.

He even did aftercare. Once he finished inside of me, he kept his semi-hard dick nestled inside of me while switching our positions so that he was on the bottom, laying me out on top. Whispering things I was too wrung out to hear, he stroked the back of my head while holding me close, cuddling in a way I never would've expected from a man with such kinks, he has to pay his partners.

Shit, after that? I should be wondering how much *he* charges?

It was the emotional connection that did it; for me, at least. Though I accused him of being a stranger when I first saw his face, once he had me under him, he was just Hunter. It didn't matter *which*. He was the charming stranger who walked me home that first night, just like he was the flirty customer who bought coffee from me even though he's not a fan.

He's Hunter—and for a little bit tonight, he was *mine*.

It's over for the moment. After making sure I was okay, he set me on the messy blanket beneath us. Once he was redressed, he tugged the skirt of my dress down so that my lower half was covered, then stood up.

He hoists himself out of the grave easily. Dropping to one knee, he offers me his hand.

Finding a drop of energy, I pull myself to my feet and take it from him.

With his help, I'm suddenly out of the grave, looking up at him.

With another one of his knowing smirks, Hunter lets go of my hand before cradling the back of my head in his. At first, his fingers run through my short hair, thumbs caressing the heights of my cheeks as he presses his sweaty brow against my forehead.

I part my lips, inviting the kiss I know he'll take anyway.

He bites down on my bottom lip, swallowing my cry when the edge of his canine splits mine down the middle.

I gasp at the jolt of pain.

He sucks my tongue into his mouth, taking complete control of the kiss.

When he's done, he narrows his eyes on me. "Too

much? I need to know how far I can take this. Take you. If that pain was too much, let me know."

I shake my head. "I'm okay. That didn't really hurt. It was more a surprise than anything."

"Just checking."

Hunter darts his tongue out, lapping at the drop of blood welling along the split in my lip.

"So fucking sweet, I swear it. Be careful, Sally. I might just devour you whole."

As he reluctantly releases me before melting into the shadows of the night, I lift my hand to my mouth. My fingertips probe my lip gently as I think to myself that—whoever he is—I might just let him.

COME OUT, COME OUT,
little doe...

HUNTER

That last taste of Sally doesn't last as long as I hoped.

I took everything she had to offer me in that grave, then set her loose again. It took everything I had not to immediately run her down, throwing her to the ground before I found my way back inside of her again.

It's where I belong. Her taste, her heat, her whimpering cries and I took her mercilessly… if I hadn't needed a little time to bounce back again, I would've flipped her onto her back already, burying myself so deep inside of her, my cock will be a part of her the way she already lives inside of my heart.

Now, I'm a healthy guy. Don't get me wrong. I'm only twenty-nine, so though my days of needing less than ten minutes to get it up again are behind me, it rarely takes me more than twenty before I've gone from limp to completely erect.

My little doe wrung every last fucking drop of come from me as I filled her up. It's been months since I've gotten laid, and though I jerked off beneath her apartment more times than I can count, I've been edging myself, too, not wanting to blow my entire load when—instinctively—I knew it already belonged to this one woman.

There was a reason I kept as much distance from her as I did. Deep down, I knew I wouldn't be satisfied with one night, and it wouldn't be long before she saw straight through to my intensity and my obsession, running off before I ever had the chance to chase after her.

So I taunted myself instead, teasing myself from the shadows, watching her and knowing that, if I ever saw her bring another guy home, I'd gut him like a fucking fish.

It's what I did to the fucker who followed her home one night, thinking that her open window was an invitation. He never saw me, hidden in the shadows just beyond the fire escape, but he barely had the chance to adjust his cock, then start up the stairs before I had him by the collar, my knife danced across his throat to silence him before I dug the point right through his belly.

I couldn't have Sally, but fuck if I was going to

stand there and let someone else take what I'd kill to have.

Only now… there'll be a hunt tonight, but it's more a sacrifice I'm making to her instead of in her name. On Halloween night, once it's dark again, I'll feed my bloodlust the same way I've given in to my body's undeniable needs.

And then, once Sally sees how devoted I am to her, maybe I'll get to do that again.

And again.

And *again*…

Licking my lips, I search for a taste of her cunt or the sweetness of her blood. It warmed me up from the inside out, making me hunger for *more*, but I know I've already pushed her too far.

The grave spooked her. The knife stole her breath. The way I savored her taste… I won't hide who I am. Not now. By insisting I take off the mask, I'm prepared to show Sally Clark exactly who Hunter Reed is.

Not the Hunter who flirted with her. Not the Hunter my more charming brother thinks that I can be when he's not being himself. I should have known that something was up when Nicholas disappeared for hours at a time, but as obsessed as I was with watching over Sally when she was vulnerable instead of trailing her to the one place she was safe—that coffee shop where she works—I figured that he was doing the same.

Who knows? After a decade since Tamryn disappeared on him, maybe he finally found someone else to have the next Reed. Because one of us had to, and we both knew it wouldn't be me.

Until now…

I've never gone bareback inside of one of my girls before. I couldn't risk it. Despite every single one being vetted before they could step on our property, it wasn't disease I was worried about, but knocking them up and being responsible for them.

I'm a killer. True to my namesake, I'm a hunter, but I'm a serial killer, too. No matter how I try to justify it—and I usually don't since I know what I am, and I'm happy about it—I've killed countless… but there's a thin line between my father and his sons.

He didn't just kill to feed his dark side. He killed because he enjoyed it and no one was safe from him. I know of at least two victims who he slaughtered because he knocked them up and he already had me and Nicholas to carry on the family name.

Shit, sometimes I wonder why he didn't off one of us. If we'd been fraternal twins, a boy and a girl instead of identical boys, he probably would've. That was how my dad was wired, and he reminded us that we only existed out of his mercy up until the day Nicholas held him down and I carved out his heart.

It was red. Squishy and slick, stuck on the rib I had to break to yank it free, fifteen-year-old me was surprised it wasn't black and shriveled and as tiny as the fucking Grinch's was from that old special Nicholas and me watched while that old bastard was out on another one of his hunts.

At least we only keep our kills to Halloween these days, and to those who deserve it.

Tonight's target? He deserves *everything* he has coming to him.

But that's not until after it's dark again. Until then, I have Sally for a couple of more hours… if I can find her.

If?

No.

When.

"Come out, come out, little doe…"

It's about half-past four when I stumble on another breather.

It's not Sally, though, and I'm impressed that she managed to evade me this long. Gotta say, it's a fucking pain in the ass to stalk through the woods, half-jogging, half-crouched so that I can slip into the shadows like this. My achy dick is hard and just about pulsing to the rhythm of my heart as all the blood rushes south, but I take my time. I can't risk her seeing me and bolting again so I jab the heel of my hand against my jeans, putting pressure against my erection, and continue to track her down.

It's Nicholas who I find first.

In case Sally managed to veer off to the edge of our property instead of running ahead like I've been herding her all along, my brother agreed to wait outside of the gate so that he'll know exactly when she tries to escape.

Normally, if it was an ordinary hunt, he'd be inside, enjoying a Scotch while watching all of the screens we have in the video room. We have cameras all over the property for obvious reasons. As much as we love having a record of some of our more brutal hunts, we have secrets we prefer to keep dead and buried, and an impressive security system helps with that.

It's true that all of Shadowvale knows to leave Reed property alone. Still, there's always some fucking idiot who thinks that it's worth the risk, sneaking onto our land. A couple of times, one of my girls thought she might be able to trigger my predator instincts on her own, hoping for a little dick and only getting Nicholas in one of his rare rages.

I know the rumors about me in town. I've earned every last lick of my reputation, but Nicholas… whenever he lashes out, I let him be Hunter.

Nicholas is the thinker. The logical bastard who does all of the planning, whether for our family businesses or our side gig dealing out our own twisted brand of justice. I'm the predator, the huntsman, the one who shows the world my dark side instead of hiding it behind a flat expression and a three-piece suit.

The cameras are off tonight. Nicholas insisted, but I would've gone back and demanded it once I saw her standing on the back porch in that pretty white dress. I don't want anyone watching me with my little doe; that's for Sally and me alone.

Tonight, he's taken up guard just outside of the gate. He told me he would the last time I checked in with him, back when I was so sure that Sally would chicken out and pull a runner. I hoped the promise of double if she stayed through Halloween night would be enough, and so far it has... but it's only four o'clock now. There's plenty of time for her to change her mind.

And even more time for me to convince her to stay...

As I approach the gate, Nicholas appears from out of the darkness, standing beneath the moon. He's changed from his business clothes to a heavy black sweater, black jeans, and black boots. Without anything covering our face, it's the only part of him that stands out from the shadows.

He raises his hand.

I acknowledge him with a nod, then wait for him to approach the gate.

It's closed, but not locked. He eases it open, then looks me up and down.

The first thing my brother asks me is, "Where's the mask?"

I lift my hand, scrubbing my face with my palm. I know why he's so surprised. My girls are always hand-picked to be those with a mask kink. They like it when they don't see my face, and I love it when they let me ravage them without them using my boyish good looks against me.

Some of the girls know the legend of Hunter Reed. Those that do, they usually know what I look like, and if not, they've seen Nicholas. It's probably why they agree to the arrangement in the first place since I'm conventionally attractive. If I was some kind of old, ugly troll under my mask, they'd have a much harder time letting me touch them no matter how much they're getting paid.

Others? Well, money fucking talks, don't it? And even if it didn't, one eyeful of my cock after I let it spring out and, suddenly, the mask doesn't matter. In fact, most of the girls get off even harder without having any clue who's got them pinned, pounding them like the only thing that counts are those fleeting moments of pleasure.

I know there are a few who wonder why I have to pay at all. They don't ask; if it ain't my business why they charge, it's not theirs when I pay them off, then tip them well. Let them think it's a toss-up between my mask kink and my need to chase them down before I take them on the grounds. If anything, they should be the ones who understand that this is just another transaction.

What I have with Sally, though?

It's different—and another reason why I allowed her to order me to take off my mask.

I've never fucked without it. I've cut it up so that I could eat pussy when I wanted to, and I've even lifted it up from the bottom when one of my girls needed a little assurance about who they were fucking, but I never removed it.

Until tonight.

"Sally found me. I told her, if she did, I'd do anything she wanted. She asked for me to take off the mask." I wait a beat and then, with a hint of pride, I tell him, "She knew I wasn't you. Identical fucking twins and she could tell us apart from a single glance."

Nicholas looks impressed. "How?"

I tap my cheek. "That beauty mark shit you got on your face. She saw I didn't have one. Knew right away I wasn't Hunter, so I had to let her know that I am."

"She understand?"

"Not at first," I admit, though that's not so surprising. If you're not Nicholas or me, it's hard to understand how we can be ourselves *and* we can be each other, but it's not like we're just swapping places. He wanted her to fall for me, so he became me, and that was that. Only... "She told me that Hunter never touched her before tonight. I'm glad to hear it. I love you, bro, but you'd be missing a couple of fingers if you tried."

"She's yours," Nicholas says simply. "I did what I had to so that she knew it, too."

And she did. Because, though the man she developed feelings for might have been Nicholas as Hunter, I'm the one who took her. Who *claimed* her. Who fucked her until she was panting my name to the stars above… and once I had her body bowed, mine covering hers… she knew exactly who Hunter Reed is.

Hers.

That settled, I ask him, "How's everything going?"

Nicholas shrugs. "I figured I'd get some work done while I guarded the gate for you. My laptop's in the car. How about you?" Peering closely at me, his expression becomes satisfied. "Better birthday than me, you bastard. You already fucked her. What happened to prolonging the chase?"

I tried. I really did. But then she found me and I had to prove that *I'm* the only Hunter who matters…

"I made it a couple of hours," I say at last. I chuckle, a laugh that only Nicholas will see the humor in. "She found me when I was checking on our target's grave."

"And?"

"And what? I figured I'd christen it before that asshole got chucked inside."

Nicholas is quiet for a moment, then he echoes my

laugh. "You sick fuck. I give you the girl of your dreams and you decide to bang her in a freshly dug grave?"

"Hey," I say, defending myself, "I put a blanket down first, just in case."

"Hunter—"

"It is what it is. Besides, she might be the girl of my dreams, but that just means I get to be her nightmare, Nick. Better she get used to that now." When my twin begrudgingly nods in agreement, I jerk my chin at him. "What about you? I appreciate it and all, but this can't be the way you want to spend your birthday."

"Don't you worry about me. I arranged for you to get laid. Don't you think I did the same for myself?"

I hadn't thought about it—but now that I am, I should've expected that response from my twin.

Now, I can go months between chases. Since meeting Sally, I hadn't even thought about getting a different woman beneath me since none of them could compare to her. Sure, I wasn't going to refuse my twin's offer before I knew it was my little doe, but all I needed tonight was the lure of our annual kill.

Nicholas, on the other hand… his red room rarely goes a couple of weeks without a guest. And it isn't so surprising that every single one of them is a brown-eyed brunette with long hair, a slender waist, and a face as heart-shaped as the one Tamryn broke when she ran off on Nicholas.

No. Not broke.

Stole.

Because while mine might be as black as I swore our father's was, Nicholas… I don't think he even has one anymore.

Case in point? When he slipped up over the summer and called one of the women he hired "Tam" right as he busted his nut inside of her.

The next morning, she was buried in a plot next to last Halloween's target.

We don't keep secrets from each other. I'm the one who grabbed the damn shovel when Nicholas told me he needed me, and I kept my fucking mouth shut when he admitted his lapse.

It was the first time in ten years I heard him say her name. And when Nicholas tried to say he killed her because she tried to pull a knife on him and rob him after sex, I accepted that—even if I wondered if that wasn't the main reason he had to slit her throat.

To cover up my suspicions, I keep the whole thing light-hearted. I teased my twin then, just like I do now.

"Good luck with this one," I tell him, reaching over to clap him on the shoulder. "Hopefully she'll make it through a night with you."

Nicholas gives me another of his flat looks. "Then she better not try to fucking rob me."

Or, in the red-tinged dark, look enough like Tamryn Carlisle to fuck with Nicholas.

Hunter Reed is a dangerous man, but a Nicholas Reed who lets himself off the chain he's been on nearly his entire life?

God bless Shadowvale and whoever sets him free because, holy shit, they're gonna need it.

Already I can see him bristling beneath the mask he forever wears. It's just not a cloth mask with a skeleton printed on it like mine… but, make no mistake, it's a mask all the same.

"Hey… you sure you want to stick around here? You could be resting up for your big date."

"I'll be fine. Besides, I can't let her slip away that easily. Not after all the trouble I went to to get her for you."

Something about Nicholas's tone has me grinning. "But I told her she could. If she found the gate… she gets the cash, and she gets to go."

"And? *You* told her that she could leave," Nicholas says, mirroring my grin. "I never did."

Ah… that's my twin.

COME OUT, COME OUT,
little doe...

SALLY

I found the gate.

I… I found it.

It's gotta be closing in on dawn. I've managed to avoid Hunter since he helped me out of the *grave* I fucked him in, but while the sky has gone from pitch-black close to purple, I know this part of the night's almost over.

To be honest, I was looking for the cabin when I passed it. Without Hunter hot on my heels, I finally realized something that I should have hours ago. If I really wanted to leave, all I had to do was find any part of the fence and follow it. Eventually it would lead me to the open gate, right?

And it did.

I could leave. It's open. I can see a gap that, even

if I don't have the strength to push past it, I could slip right through. I gave Hunter what he wanted, and I'm so damn exhausted I'm ready to find a spot to curl up in if I can't locate the cabin he handed me a key to at the beginning of the night, but I stare at the gate and then… I don't know.

I keep on going.

Four grand, I tell myself. Four grand and another chance to use Hunter's body the same way he seems more than happy to use mine.

At least I know for sure that the man I let go down on me, the man I went to all fours for in a freaking *grave* really is Hunter Reed.

Does that make me feel any better that the man *I* knew as Hunter Reed really is his twin? Or that, all this time, everyone seemed happy to mention that the two were brothers, but no one ever said, "Hey. They're twins?"

Nope.

Does that change anything? If this Hunter wanted a night with me so bad that his twin decided to play the part to catch my attention, I might as well let him have it.

For four grand, I'm not above letting him have anything he wants—especially since, despite knowing all this, I still can't resist the pull I feel toward him.

Obviously.

So, mentally clocking where I saw the gate in case

I change my mind and have to make an escape quicker than midnight tonight, I keep running.

He told me that the game pauses when the sun comes up. Whether it's because he's a vampire or he has business to take care of in the daylight hours, your guess is as good as mine, but I decide that it pauses when I find the cabin.

I've got a key. Hoping it's the only one, I'll find it and lock myself in it until I'm ready to face Hunter again.

Face him… who am I kidding? If he catches me, he's going to fuck me. And if, by some miracle, I catch him again?

I… I'm going to fuck him.

And that's exactly what happens.

I don't find him. I wish I had because then, at least, I would've been in charge, but just as I'm heading back toward the main house in the distance, searching for the cabin, he appears again, snagging my hand before I can even turn in the other direction.

That was my fault. I remembered too late that he said the cabin was located about an acre off from the house. Now, I'm a city girl. I know fuck all about acres, but it seems like it's probably much closer to the big house than it is to the far edge of the fence where I found the exit to their property.

So consumed with finding it before sun-up, as if that was another part of our game I had to play, I thought I might have been heading the right way—

hoping I'd stumble on the cabin before he stumbled upon me—when, suddenly, he has me in his arms again.

I'm used to being manhandled by him by now. He treats me like his little doll, though he calls me his 'little doe', and though he's pressing hot-opened mouth kisses to my throat that have me melting right against him, he doesn't set me down again until he has my back up against a tree.

Once again, I'm stuck between a rock and a hard place. Only, in this case, the rock is the massive oak tree behind me. And the hard place? Is Hunter's hard chest—and even harder cock.

"Miss me, Sally? That's the longest it took me to find you."

I jut my chin out at him. There's no mask anymore, probably because he has nothing to hide any longer, and it takes everything I have not to be dazzled by his face. "Maybe I'm getting better at your game."

"You are," he agrees. "But… hey, you're not done playing with me, are you?"

Good question.

I'm filthy. I have grass in my hair, dirt on my knees, and the white dress that Hunter—or Hunter's twin—gave me to wear is a lost cause. The grave dirt marks most of the fabric, especially since Hunter insisted on me wearing it while he fucked me in the grave, and despite the chilly air, I sweated all over the damn thing. So did he. It smells like sex and earth and Hunter fucking Reed, and no matter what happens come midnight tonight, I know deep down that I'll keep the simple slip dress as a memento.

I'm *exhausted*. I'm running on a combination of adrenaline and desire, and the only reason I didn't pass out after he made me come was because—in the back of my mind—I never forgot that I was in a *grave*. He tossed me in and had his body covering mine faster than I could scramble back out of it, but as much as I've given up to have Hunter tonight, I drew the line at willingly falling asleep in a freshly dug grave.

I'm sticky, I'm hungry, and my body is so sensitized right now that the thought of him touching me has me torn between flinching away from him and throwing myself at him again.

And yet...

"No," I answer honestly.

I'm addicted. Hunter Reed is like coffee to me, something I can't live without, and the one thing that gives me the energy to go on.

"That's my girl." His hand goes to my throat, collaring me in place as he shoves his knees between my thighs, spreading them open.

I swallow. His hand tightens, but I'm not nervous.

Oh, no.

I'm turned *on*.

"I thought I was your 'little doe'."

"You are, baby. My sweet Sally, too. See a theme? You're all things *mine*."

"For Halloween," I dare him.

He smirks. "If that's all I get, I better make it count."

Without releasing my throat, he uses his free hand to unbuckle his belt. My breathing picks up when I hear his zipper; like I'm Pavlov's fucking dog or something, I hear the sound and immediately start creaming myself, getting ready for his dick.

My back is getting scraped the hell up as he pushes me against the rough bark. Again, this tiny bit of pain triggers something else inside of me, twisting my gut to the point that I'm half ready to come by the time he squats low enough to find my pussy.

One thrust. That's all it takes. One thrust into my waiting pussy and he's fully seated. Freeing me for only a heartbeat, he lifts me up again so that my legs are secured around his waist, the tree supporting my back as he starts to fuck me.

There's something different about this time. As though he really thinks this might be our last time together, he pistons his hips, not even trying to hide the fact that he's chasing his nut.

Me? I'm just here for the ride—at least, that's what I think until he collars my throat again, cutting off my air.

I've never done erotic asphyxiation before. I've heard of it, yeah, that cutting off your breath during sex or masturbation increases the high and makes you come like you wouldn't believe.

Is that what he's doing now?

Maybe… but, then again, this is Hunter Reed.

His jeans shoved down past his ass, his cock moving so quickly, I'm pinned on its length as he alternates between thrusting and rocking but never quite pulling out of me as though he can't bear the separation, he's fucking me—and he's choking me, too.

"I could kill you," he whispers, as conversational as if discussing what he plans on dressing up for Halloween later tonight. "Turn you into my hunt instead of my chase. Squeeze your throat until everything went black… and you'd let me, wouldn't you?"

What?

Everything is already kind of turning black. On the edge of my vision, it's a little bit fuzzy, but there's no denying that—at the same time—all of my other senses are heightened.

I struggle to lift my hand, trying to pull on his. "Hun… Hunter. *Please.*"

He doesn't squeeze any tighter, though he doesn't let go, either. "I should. Maybe if you were in that grave I'd find a way to get you out of my head. Tasting you made it worse. Fucking you has me thinking thoughts you don't want to know. And here I am, finding solace in your pussy, and salvation in your doe eyes."

He leans down, pressing his forehead to mine. "My little doe… everything about you calls to me. It mocks me but in all the best ways. But if you died? No one on this fucking planet would be safe from me and my rage. Kill you? No way. I'd sooner take my knife and carve out my own damn heart than see you get hurt."

Hunter drops his hand, thumbing my hard nipple through my dress. That little bit of stimulation after his confession—and the way his hold on my throat had me on the edge of losing consciousness for a moment there—has me exploding around him.

He follows close behind. Almost like my coming was a sign that he could let go, too, right when I start squeezing him, tightening my legs around him like a freaking anaconda, he grunts out my name—*Sally*—before filling me up with his come.

Only once he's sure that I've taken every drop does he help disentangle my quivering legs from around his body.

I collapse against him.

Hunter holds me tight. "Did I hurt you?"

"You frightened me," I admit, whispering into his chest.

"Don't be. I meant it when I said I won't ever let anyone hurt you. That includes me, little doe."

I'm dozy. Lightheaded, too, and pretty damn boneless from what he just did to me, plus I'm as weak as a kitten, too feeble to do anything but allow him to settle me across his lap after he stretches out beneath the tree.

"Mm." That's about all I can muster right now.

"What's that?"

"Just… why do you keep calling me 'little doe'?"

He lifts his hand, using two fingers to shut my eyelids. I leave them closed, snuggling up against him as he says, "It's the way you first looked at me. The real me. Like an adorable deer in headlights, especially with those big brown eyes of yours. I was hooked from that moment on. That's when you became my 'little doe'." His hand goes to the top of my head, his fingers running through my sweat-soaked strands. "That's when you became mine."

For one night, I think.

But I don't say it out loud.

I can't.

I'm already fast asleep.

COME OUT, COME OUT,
little doe...

HUNTER

Just as the sun begins to brighten the sky, Sally slips free from my arms and dashes away.

That's on me. After I took her that second time, I let my guard down with Sally clinging to me so sweetly. Half asleep, drunk on power and pleasure, I was thinking about saying 'fuck it' and carrying her off to my bed.

There's never been a woman who meant enough to me to spend a night there. I fucked where I pleased, but I kept my room off-limits. It's my territory. I always knew I'd never invite anyone into it unless they were going to stay.

I want to keep Sally. Chained to the foot of my fucking bed if I have to, now that I've discovered how deliciously sweet she is, I have to admit that I'm not just obsessed. I'm truly *addicted*. I went from watching her, fantasizing about slipping into her apartment, climbing into her bed and making her mine… but, thanks to my twin, I didn't have to take what she so freely offered him when she thought he was me.

But he *was* me. Using my name, my mannerisms, my everything… it was Hunter who hungered for her, and it's Hunter who will do whatever it fucking takes to keep her.

You ask me, the game was over the moment she got on her hands and knees, arching her back as she presented her ass and her pussy to me. I could have taken either one and she would have let me. I fucked her in a *grave* and she didn't even seem to notice as the dirt rained down on us.

I've pushed my girls to their limits before. Bending them over headstones, forcing them to their knees in the shadow of the stone angels of century-old graves, fucking them on trampled grass as twigs and leaves got tangled up in their styled hair. For what my body could give them—and however much I was paying them for their obedience—they took it all… but I never forgot for a fucking moment that they were paid-for pussy, letting me chase them, then use them because I made it worth their while.

But my little doe… Nicholas put two thousand dollars on the table. To give her incentive, to prove to myself that I was wasting my obsession on someone who could never love me the way I can't breathe without her, I doubled it.

And then I fucked her that first time as though it might be my last, reminding her that she was being paid well for her pussy,

I tried to make her my whore. But Sally... she's more than that.

She's *mine*.

Balls deep as she pushed back against me... that's when I knew. Whether she just momentarily blanked on our terms or she's inexplicably drawn to me the same way I have been since I followed her home that fateful night, it doesn't matter. I'll give her as much as she wants so that she'll never have to work again, that she can give up that shithole apartment and stay with me forever, but after this Halloween... I'll never let her get away.

Of course, just as I promise myself that, I relax up against the tree and close my eyes, loosening my hold on her.

My skittish prey doesn't hesitate to escape.

I should have expected that. I claimed Sally, fucking her in the grave I plan on using for my target later tonight, and then held her close, finding almost as much pleasure wearing her on my lap as I did, nutting as deep inside of her as I could. But at no time did I tell her that she's mine, or get off my ass to carry her inside.

I never let her know the chase is over. I caught her,

I claimed her, and now she's *mine*—and she doesn't know it.

Let her wash me off of her. Let her try to run again. I've filled her up so completely that no matter what, I've reached parts of her that no one ever will again.

I'll make sure of it, too—even if she used her head start to run for the gate. Even if she escapes the Reed House, even if she tries to pull a Tamryn and leave Shadowvale… there isn't anywhere I won't follow her.

Sorry, sweet Sally. With the first part of the night over, it's time to change the rules of our little game…

Pushing up off of the ground, I get to my feet. The early morning chill has seeped into my bones, leaving me stiff in more ways than one. After dropping my hand, checking to see that I still have my knife in its holster, I crack my neck, stretching it out. My back aches from holding her up as I pounded into her before using the tree as something to lean up against. Giving a quick twist, I work the kink out, then roll my head on my neck.

My blood's pumping. I only managed to pull my jeans up over my ass after I finished before. Without zipping my cock up it in my pants, it was tucked beneath Sally's ass. Now that she's gone, I noticed that she left me hard and ready to work myself inside her tight snatch again.

Silly girl. If it wasn't for dawn breaking, I'd hunt

her down now and make her take care of my erection with her pretty mouth. She'll soon learn that, if she gets my cock pumping, it'll be on her to take care of it.

For everything she'll ever want, that's all I'll ask for in return. Well, her loyalty, too, but a lifetime of being worshipped by a fucking Reed in exchange for her loyalty and her getting me off whenever I want… that seems fair enough to me.

It has to be her, too. From the moment she opened up to me, taking every last inch I had to offer, my cock belongs to her now. She already had my heart in her hands… now she has the rest of me.

Whether she wants it or not.

My cock belongs to Sally, but with her gone, I quickly rub one out. I mark the dirt beneath the tree where I took Sally, then place my palm against my nose, breathing in deep. I'm still coated in her scent, and most of it transferred to my skin with the vigorous stroking.

It smells *delicious*.

I hunger for her. I crave her in a way that's probably not natural, but that seems perfectly right to a twisted bastard like me.

Invigorated by breathing her into my lungs like that—not to mention how much better I feel after nutting again—I tuck my cock into my jeans, zip up, and start to jog.

The one downside to having the cameras off is that I don't have a way of knowing where Sally ran off to. My head says one thing, my gut another, and my black heart tells me that it doesn't matter. Wherever she is, I'll find her, and if I have to drug her and carry her back here, I will.

And Nicholas will help me.

I owe my twin. Not only for arranging this tonight, or understanding why we don't have a video feed going. Because this night with Sally was mine, Nicholas—who is Nicholas again—did something I've never been able to do when it comes to him and his life: he stayed out of it.

But, for the same reason, he went ahead and parked one of his more discreet, black coupes about twenty feet away from the gate on our property, his laptop propped up on his lap as he kept an eye on his work *and* the closed doorway. I can tell it's on from the slight glow illuminating his face, though even from this distance, Nicholas is watching the gate closely.

It's not locked. I'd meant what I said earlier, that I'd give Sally every chance to escape. This gate is the only way off of the property that my little doe will ever be able to find, but because we both—Nicholas and I—knew that I'd never actually be able to let her go, he's been guarding over it all night while I had my fun.

I told her she could escape. But my twin… like he pointed out earlier, he never did, did he?

Shit, I owe him. Maybe not this birthday, but I'm going to give him the one thing he's always wanted for giving me mine—even if he'd rather I stayed out of it.

Pushing the gate open, I stalk toward the car. At the same time, Nicholas pops open the door, climbing out of the car and standing up on the side so that his head appears over the top.

I don't even have to ask. Our eyes lock and Nicholas shakes his head.

"She didn't come out this way, Hunter. Ran by it once, maybe thought about it for a second, but she kept on going."

The relief that rushes through me is pathetic. I wanted her to *want* to stay, even if only until the end of Halloween, but I expected my little doe to have scampered through the gate the first chance she got.

That she didn't? To me, that's further proof that she was meant for me the same way I was born to make her mine.

I spent months… *months*… trying to be a fucking Reed. Going back more than a hundred years, the pricks in my line indulge their dark side by filling up the graveyard on our family land, only using a pussy for pleasure and to continue popping out more Reeds.

I've got no sisters. No aunts. No cousins at all. No mother, and considering my monster of a father got off on killing women weaker than him, I wouldn't be surprised if she's in one of the unmarked plots he filled up before me and Nicholas took care of him.

After what happened with Tamryn, Nicholas became like every other Reed. Fuck a woman when his hand didn't cut it any longer, but don't get attached. I wanted to be like my older brother. Paying for pussy made it a transaction, with no strings attached and no chance of catching feelings.

And then I met Sally, and I wanted.

Fuck did I *want.*

I still do. One look in her doe eyes, haunted and innocent and hypnotizing… the shy smile she offered me as I walked her home, too naive and innocent to know she was walking side by side with death… the way something about her called to the darkness inside of me… I knew she was too good to be just another lay.

But what else could I offer her? Reeds don't get married. They don't have forever.

We sure as hell don't get a 'happily ever after'…

Then again, maybe I'll just have to be the first.

Nicholas jerks his chin at me. "You ready for tonight?"

Ready to show Sally that there isn't anything I won't do for her?

"Yeah. You?"

"I'm going to pick him up around four. Should be back by seven or so."

"That late?" I ask my twin. That doesn't give me

much time with him if I want to enjoy Sally a little more.

Nicholas scowls. With that expression, my identical twin looks more like me than he usually does. "I didn't want to tip off the target we had eyes on him. If he ran, we'd be fucked, and not in the way that has you smirking, Hunter. It was either agree to meet him at four or you wouldn't get your kill tonight."

He's right, too. This year, it was Nicholas's turn to pick the target while I got to finish them off. Now that he showed me the guy's picture, no way I can settle for anyone else.

"Fine," I tell him. "But we're still having dinner, right?"

"Of course." His scowl kicks up into a grin. "It's tradition." Tapping the roof of his car, he adds, "You want me to take a different car, leave this one here for you to keep an eye out? Or do you want to put the cameras back on while I'm gone, watch her from there?"

I promised Sally a pause in our little game. I said I would only chase her while it's dark, giving her time to rest if she didn't escape before the sun came up, and that's not something I'm prepared to go back on.

So if she didn't take the chance to leave while she could, I hope she found the cabin as easily as she did the gate…

"Don't worry about it. If I know my little doe,

she's right where I want her. And where I'm gonna keep her... for today, at least."

After that? I'll move her into our house, one way or another.

Nicholas nods. "You better go check. I'll give it fifteen and if you don't come back, I'll meet you at the house. I gotta get ready for my drive, and my date. Yeah?"

I guess my twin decided he wanted to go ahead with celebrating our birthday the way he prefers. Here's hoping that he doesn't pick tonight to lose control again.

Way things have gone so far, who knows what will happen if we both do?

"Yeah," I tell him. "Sounds good."

***

JUST LIKE I THOUGHT, SALLY IS IN MY CABIN.

This part of the property is mine. Nicholas has his red room inside of the house. Me? I keep this small space for when I have one of my girls over. In case they need a place to rest and recover since I've never let any of them enter our home.

I gave her a key so she could let herself inside. Peering through the side window, watching as she moves around the single-room cabin, once again completely oblivious to the fact that I've got my eyes on her, I resist the urge to pull out my cock again.

Later, I promise myself.

Until then, I slip past the window, approaching the front door.

If Sally was smart, she would've locked the cabin up tight once she found her way inside—and she did.

But if she was smarter? She never would've found sanctuary in the small structure, especially when she caught the attention of a monster.

Without the mask to hide my grin, I smile widely to no one as I engage the additional lock at the top of the door. This way, no one can get in—and no one can get out.

At least, not until I'm ready to chase her again…

COME OUT, COME OUT,
little doe...

5:58 PM

SALLY

Falling asleep earlier this morning was a whole lot easier than I thought it would be, all things considered.

Not like I hopped right into the bed Hunter promised me I'd find inside. I almost wanted to, and I was so exhausted as the last of my adrenaline crashed that I was dragging my bare feet as I closed the door behind me, locking up the cabin. My body was tired yet electric and alive from everything Hunter had done to it, and if it was only his sweat and scent clinging to my skin, I wouldn't have worried about it.

But it wasn't. Dirt from the freshly dug grave was smeared all over my body. The blanket at the bottom shifted beneath me, getting dirt in my hair, too, and other places I don't want to think about.

My inner thighs were sticky from where he came inside of me. All night I've been getting a pit in my stomach whenever I think about how he dug his fingers into my hips, bottoming out inside of me so there was nowhere else for his come to go. He seemed proud of himself, looking at his creampie with an expression of pure ownership before scooping me up, helping me out of the grave, and settling me on his lap.

My Plan B is in my purse. I'm so glad I thought to buy one at the drugstore before coming over. Something about the Hunter I got to know—who isn't even Hunter, though I guess he *pretended* to be—made me suspect he'd expect his lovers to take him as he was. In any other situation, I would've insisted on a condom, but after being chased and taken, pleasured and *claimed* tonight… it didn't cross my mind until I was away from Hunter, probing my pussy as I thought about what I'd already let him do.

What I'll probably let him do *again* once the sun finishes setting since I purposely headed for the cabin instead of my freedom off of it…

I don't have my bag with me. Following "Hunter"'s instructions, I left it in my car, figuring I'd be able to run out to it and grab it if I needed it. With it parked on Reed land, I was assured I wouldn't have to worry about anyone breaking into my shitty car, so my keys are there, too.

It makes sense now that I know what kind of

game the Reed brothers—the Reed *twins*—like to play. Once I find my way off of their land, I could hop in my car and get as far away from this Halloween night as I can.

I know where the exit is. I passed it by accident. If I was smart, I would've fled through the gate. If I had, I could've left right before dawn and been home by the time the sun was up… but, instead, I went to the cabin hidden at the edge of the graveyard.

Four thousand dollars is a lot of money. That's what Hunter promised me. If I can escape the graveyard by midnight at the end of Halloween, he'll double what his twin offered me. I want it… but there's something addictive about being his prey tonight. Like there isn't anything he wouldn't do for me…

No one has ever looked at me like that before. Behind his mask, it was easy to miss the lust… the obsession… the *need* in his pretty blue eyes. Once I got him to remove it, I felt like I was the only one in the world who existed for him.

It's just for Halloween. He—whichever *he* he was—asked me for one night. Come November 1st, I don't know what will happen or what to expect, but so long as it's Halloween, I'm his.

And I… I kind of want to be.

Just like he promised, the cabin has everything I need to ready myself for the second part of Halloween night. A single shower stall, a refrigerator that's gotta be hooked up to the generator behind the small structure, a fresh bed, and a new white dress laid out on the covers.

It's exactly the same as the one I had on before. A pair of flats is tucked by the door, I notice, and somehow I'm not even a little surprised to find that they are my size.

Did he know I would choose to go here? Was this just a gamble of his? And the shoes… he's the one who noticed I kicked off my heels so I could run faster. Were these always here or is this something he arranged in between chasing me through the grave-yard and the trees?

I don't know, but it doesn't matter, does it? They're here, and after I'm refreshed, I'm taking them with me.

Once I made the decision to stay a little longer, the first thing I did was take a nice, hot shower to chase the chill from my bones. After drying off, I pulled on the new dress, then finger-combed my short hair before turning to the fridge.

The white flats in my size surprised me, but I gaped when I saw all of the different types of food waiting for me in the fridge. From the brand of the lemonade on the top shelf to my preferred diet soda on the second, and the snack cakes I eat when my sweet tooth gets out of control, they're my favorites. So are the box of crackers on the counter, the bag of chips, and the green box of cookies that remind me of my childhood.

It's like all my guilty pleasures in one place. Like Hunter made it his mission to learn about what I love to snack on so that I would have something to eat in case I worked up an appetite. There's healthy shit in here, too, but as though he could guess what I would grab, I went right for one of the snack cakes before I curled up on the bed.

I don't know how long I slept for when I finally knocked out. Hours definitely, but without my phone or any kind of clock in here, I have no idea. Hunter told me that he'll only chase me when it's dark out, so I figured I'd have to wait until the sun goes down before I'll see him again.

With nothing else to do, I slept, and when I woke up again and reality set in—when it really hit me that everything that happened last night *did* happen and could easily happen *again*—I lost my nerve and bolted for the door.

At first, I thought I was messing up the lock. When the doorknob didn't turn under my hand no matter how much I rattled it, my attention went straight to the lock. I twisted it one way, then the other, pausing only to jimmy the doorknob again—but it was stuck.

No.

Not stuck.

It was locked—just not on the inside.

The windows were a decoration. I knew that because I tested them before, relieved when I found they were sealed shut; I wouldn't have slept at all if I thought anyone—even Hunter—could sneak in when I was at my most vulnerable. But now I have to admit that I was safer than I thought.

No one can get in… but I can't get out.

The first time I hear the phone ringing, I jump.

The cabin is quiet. If I concentrate, I can pick up the gentle hum of the generator outside, but I've gotten used to it over the last hour or two. The chime is one of those stock ringtones that come with any phone, but I wasn't expecting it and I jump when it goes off.

My heart pounding in my chest, it takes a second or two for me to recognize the sound. By the time I've scrambled out of the bed, searching for the source of the ring, it's died… only to start up again a moment later.

It takes me another call before I trace the ringing sound to one of the drawers I overlooked in the cozy kitchen part of the cabin. Yanking it open, I pull out the phone and stare at it for a moment.

There are numbers on the screen instead of a programmed contact. It doesn't say anything about a spam risk like mine does, but that doesn't mean this call could be for me. I mean, I'm locked in a cabin after spending a night with a gorgeous psycho with a thing for masks and who knows a lot more about me than I obviously do him… and who am I kidding?

Gulping, I answer the phone.

"Hello?"

"Ah, my sweet, sweet Sally," purrs a familiar voice. "I've missed you."

Hunter.

There goes that pit in my stomach again. Only… I don't think it's nerves making me feel like this right now. It's more like *anticipation*—

I gulp, squeezing the phone. "You know where I am. You locked me in here."

"I had business to take care of," he says, not even bothering to deny it. "It's Halloween. If I couldn't watch you, I needed you somewhere safe and sound until it's time to… mmm… play some more."

Safe and sound, huh? But what if the biggest danger to me is *him*?

"What if I'm done?" I ask. "What if I'm ready to go?"

"You could've escaped at any point," he reminds me.

Does he know? Does he know that I stumbled upon the gate and kept on running?

My tongue darts out. I lick my bottom lip, then ask, "What about now?" I pull the phone away from my face, glancing at the time. "It's six o'clock."

Crossing over to the window, I pull the curtain back, peering out into the woods. "It's getting dark out." The shadows are already thickening… "How can I play if you locked me in here?"

Hunter's chuckle is husky and rich. "Tell me, little doe… does that mean you're ready for me to catch you again?"

If I catch you, I get to do whatever I want…

He's already fucked me in a freshly dug grave. He licked my blood straight from his knife, he choked me enough to have me seeing sparks in front of my eyes, and he bent me over a gravestone before burying his face in my pussy.

What will happen the next time he catches me?

Am I ready?

"Yes," I lie.

"Good. Because, I fucking promise you, my sweet Sally, I'm not even a little bit close to being done with you and that even sweeter pussy of yours."

I squeeze my legs together. The silky material of the dress slides between my thighs, reminding me of Hunter's gentle touch before he used his knife to slice my panties right off of me.

If I dipped my fingers inside of me, I'd be a sopping mess. I just know it. Hunter does that to me, and maybe I'm not ready to spend the rest of Halloween fleeing past the trees, darting through the headstones while waiting for him to jump out and scare the shit out of me… but if he stalked into the cabin and ordered me to climb back into bed with him?

That's a different story, isn't it?

"Like I said, you know where to find me," I say, a daring note creeping its way into my voice. "And we both know what happens if you do."

Hunter's breath becomes a rasp. "Don't tease me, Sally. You won't like the man you provoke if you do."

"I'm not teasing."

"Yeah? Remember that, then. When I find you again… remember you said that."

Find me again?

"Aren't you going to let me out?" I ask him.

"Eventually," is his coy answer. "There are snacks in the kitchen. Rest up, little doe. You'll need it."

I know. "Hunter? You… you're not going to leave me in here the rest of the night, are you? Look." I jab my pointer finger at the window as though he can see the same things I am. "It's dark. Even if you don't want me anymore, you can't leave me here. I can't escape before midnight if I can't leave the cabin—"

"Oh, Sally… you're assuming I want you to leave me. But maybe, now that I've had you, I'm thinking about keeping you. What about that?"

My lips part as I struggle to come up with a response.

He said—

He *said*—

He said I *could* escape. He never said that I *would*.

"Hunter—"

"Less than six hours to midnight," he says in a low voice. "Keep the phone close. I'll let you know when I'm ready."

Ready? Ready for what?

"Hunter, *please*—"

"I'm doing this for you," is all he says before the phone goes dead.

For me? What is *that* supposed to mean?

I don't know, and I'm not sure when I will. And yet, as I lower the phone to my thigh, torn between excitement and fear, I can't help but admit that I don't regret my decision.

I could've escaped—but I didn't.

And now I have less than six hours to decide if I want to… or if being kept by Hunter Reed would be as enticing as it sounds.

COME OUT, COME OUT,
little doe...

8:01 PM

SALLY

I call Hunter's number more than forty times before I force myself to stop.

At least, I assume it's his number. It hits me that I agreed to this madness without even having any way to reach him, and that—like a dope—I left my phone back in my car with my purse so even if I *did* have it, I wouldn't have been able to call him.

I don't call anyone else, either. I mean, who could I call? My parents? My friends back home? My co-worker Kelsey, who would just tell me "I told you so" even if I had any idea what her number was?

How would I explain *this*?

I can't. Obviously. Besides, I gave my word that I'd keep this between the Hunters and me when I agreed to take his two grand. After everything I've done so far tonight… I'll be taking this night to my grave.

If I don't end up in one first…

Nice thought, Sally. Just because his family has a private cemetery in his backyard and he fucked you in a freshly dug hole, that doesn't mean you'll end up a victim by the end of Halloween instead of four grand richer.

Right?

Right…

Either way, none of that matters while Hunter has me locked up, waiting for him to be "ready". Desperate to get out, I kept redialing the same number over and over again, hoping he'd answer. Not only does he refuse to, but he doesn't even hit the "F-U" button or send me to voicemail. He just lets it ring and ring and ring.

I finally realize that he must've called the phone he keeps in the cabin for nights like this, then tossed his. Maybe it was a burner, or maybe he's so "busy" with whatever he's doing, there's no time for him to placate me.

Of course not. Like he said, he has me right where he wants me.

I passed the last two hours—once I gave up obsessively calling him—trying not to think about what Hunter is doing now that it's dark. I convinced myself that even psychos need their rest. While I was sleeping, he had to be doing the same in his big house.

But it's dark out. And, well, there's no denying he was surprised to see me last night. Now I know that it was his twin who spent the last few months flirting with me at Thanks a Latte because Hunter—the real Hunter, and the Reed brother who I met that first night—had kept his distance, thinking he might be too much for me.

I… he's not wrong. Not really. I made it this far, but when I think about what else he could have in store for me… I don't know.

I also don't know if he had other plans for Halloween in place before his brother invited me over.

It's clear now that Nicholas Reed arranged this—all of this—for Hunter. Hunter admitted as much himself, telling me that he'd always considered me his, and that Nicholas pretended to be him to get close to me.

But what if Hunter has another girl out there, playing his game?

And why does the thought that he might be bending her over a gravestone right about now have me burning up with jealousy?

One night. Both Hunters promised me just one night, and I'd have to be insane to think that I might want more than that. As it is, I should be upset about how "Hunter" betrayed me, making me think he was his brother. I should be even more upset that my Hunter locked me in his cabin while he's out there doing who knows what—and who knows *who*—while

I sit and wait and break a fingernail or two trying to get that damn window up.

I've never been claustrophobic before.

Tonight?

I just want out of the cabin.

Crazily enough, I want to *run*.

It doesn't occur to me to ignore Hunter's latest command. I keep the phone close, willing it to ring. After searching the cabin again, I wasn't able to find a charger. I blew through half the battery with all my earlier frantic dialing, and I decide to conserve what's left so I don't miss Hunter's call.

That means going online is out. Same with distracting myself by finding a game or something to play. I do use a good ten percent snooping through the phone, but this must be a burner, too, because it has nothing on it prior to Hunter's call at 5:58.

It's 8:01. We're down to under four hours, and I'm beginning to believe he's not letting me out—and that's when the phone finally rings again.

With trembling fingers, I pick it up off of the bed. I answer, then place it to my ear.

"Hello?"

"The hunt is on. Come and find me if you dare, little doe."

And... he's hung up on me again.

This time, I don't bother trying to call him back. Instead, dropping the phone to the bed again, I scramble out of it until I'm standing. Tripping over my bare feet, I hurry for the door.

I grab the knob, my heart thudding wildly as it turns under my hand. With a pull, the door swings inward, the dark graveyard beckoning me.

I gasp, then slam the door shut. My fingers fumble, locking the cabin from the inside now.

How did he do it? I'd been unceremoniously peeking out of the window for hours, hoping for some sign that Hunter was approaching, but he must've slipped out of the shadows, then disappeared without me having any idea.

I can leave. These last two hours at his mercy were rough, and I promised myself that I would bolt for the gate the first chance I got.

But then Hunter… he taunted me.

Come and find me if you dare…

If *I* dare?

No. It's not if *I* dare, not when he dared me first.

Hunter's not coming after me. That much is obvious. *The hunt is on…* it's not a chase anymore, is it?

He wants me to find him—and, if I do, that means it's my turn to decide what happens next.

Do I want that? Do I want him?

Or do I want to escape while I can?

Bending low, I grab the pair of flats. Whatever I choose, one thing for sure: it'll be a lot easier for me to run with these on—

Run, run, little doe…
—and that's exactly what I'm going to do.

COME OUT, COME OUT,
little doe...

9:13 PM

SALLY

I swear I heard screaming.

It was only the one time, right after I stepped foot outside of the cabin, but it was enough to send shivers up my spine as I started off.

At first, I avoided the direction that the scream came from. That's my belated sense of self-preservation kicking in, I guess, but after what seems like forever, moving quickly through the graves, searching for some sign of Hunter… I admit to myself that, if I want to find him after all, I'll have to head that way.

I lose track of how long it's been. Almost immediately, I regret leaving the phone behind. I didn't think I would need it, and I'd hop in that grave myself to save Hunter the trouble before I called the cops for help. Only after I get far enough away do I realize that, with it, I would've at least known the time.

It's dark. I'm disoriented, but I'm determined, and when I finally follow my gut and head back toward the grave where I saw Hunter last, I'm not so surprised to find him waiting for me there.

I'm not surprised to see Hunter—but the bound and gagged man sitting at his feet?

I freeze. I promised myself when I left that I would never have to come face to face with Max Casey again, but there he is. Wearing that same white hoodie that he always did, his normally shaggy hair plastered to his head, eyes wide with fright as he meets my gaze.

He makes a noise. Thanks to the gag, it's unintelligible, but I can only guess what he's saying.

Help me.

Save me.

You stupid bitch…

Hunter kicks him. One solid boot to the ribs that has Max jerking, then bowing over, his head slumped to his chest.

"Sally's our guest of honor, asshole. Didn't you learn your lesson earlier to keep your mouth fucking shut until I tell you to?"

He moves his hand. It's a quick gesture, a stab in the air out of frustration, but when the moon glances off of the blade he's clutching, I realize that it basically *was* a stab.

Because that… that's his knife, and from the scene I walked in on—Max all tied up, Hunter standing over him, the grave right by their side—it's obvious what Hunter meant when he called me the 'guest of honor'.

He was waiting for me to see this.

He was waiting for me to see the true Hunter Reed.

I lift my hand, fingers covering my mouth as I breathe out, "The rumors are true."

He doesn't ask me what I mean. I'm sure he's heard them all, just like the stories that people go up to the Reed House never to return are ones I've been told plenty of times during my four months in Shadowvale.

I just… I didn't think they were true.

But how can I deny them now?

He certainly doesn't try.

"I'm a hunter. You've always known that." He slips his knife back into the leather holster at his waist, showing off his empty hands when he's done. That doesn't fool me, though. I know how quick he can be to draw his weapon. "But I play games, too, sweet Sally. And, fuck me, I play to *win*."

Games… he told me once he liked to play games. Or his twin did. That Hunter liked to play games, to run, to hunt…

Well. He wasn't lying, was he?

"What kind of game is this?" I ask him. "What

did you do to him? Why is he wearing that around his mouth?"

"The gag?" At my frantic nod, Hunter sighs. "He said the nastiest things about you. Well, he *tried*. After the first time, I had Nicholas pin his arms and help me screw open this fucker's jaw." Just like I thought, he's quick to pull his knife back out. He shows it off to me, twisting the blade, grinning at it. "Hard to talk shit without a tongue."

Oh my God.

"Besides," Hunter says, gentling his voice as if he knows I'm seconds away from freaking the fuck out, "he's the reason you cut your pretty hair. Think of this as his sacrifice."

My hand shoots to my head. I can't help it. My fingers thread through the short strands of my pixie cut.

How does he know that? When I moved to Shadowvale, I had already cut my shoulder-length hair as short as it could go. No one here knows me with long hair, and I scrubbed all of my social media one night in a wine-fueled rage.

I shouldn't be surprised. Hunter… he knows more about me than anyone I've ever met.

Which is why he should've known that Max is a trigger for me, that I'd wished that bastard dead myself hundreds of times, but *this*… I never expected *this*.

"I found you."

Hunter's lips twitch. "You did. And that means you get something from me. What's that? Do you want me to spare him? To show him the mercy you didn't get? Is that what you're asking of me, little doe?"

Am I?

I… I don't know.

So I simply say, "He doesn't deserve this."

"Oh? Do you really think so?"

No. "Yes."

Hunter *tsks*. "He cheated on you. He stole every fucking cent you have, and when you confronted him, he put you in the hospital."

My stomach tightens. I'm still not looking at Max, keeping all of my attention on Hunter as he lays out the last year of my life so succinctly, I flinch as though each of his words hurts as much as Max's blows had.

Hunter notices.

He gentles his voice further, though he doesn't stop as he says, "He grabbed you by the hair, fisting the strands, holding you down so he could beat the shit out of you, hurting you so damn badly that the first thing you did after you left was cut it all off so you could move on… and you're going to tell me he doesn't deserve everything he has coming?"

He waves the hand with the knife, gesturing angrily at the other blank headstones surrounding us. "Just like they deserved what happened to them, too."

I tremble. When he pointed out earlier that only a

small amount of the gravestones have a Reed's name on them, I tried not to think about what that meant for all of the rest of the other ones.

I liked being in denial—but, right now, it looks like Hunter's ready to rip another mask off. A figurative one this time instead of literal, but as he stalks toward me, leaving Max on the ground, I'm forced to face this side of Hunter Reed.

His voice is still low, his touch easy as he lays his hands on my shoulders. The knife is gone, though I haven't forgotten for a moment that it's in his reach.

"Didn't you wonder why we played our game of hide and seek in a graveyard? These aren't the graves of my family. They're the graves of my prey."

I meet the fanaticism in his formerly soft blue eyes. They're hard now, *insane*, and yet… they're full of so much affection for me, I don't pull away from him.

As if he would let me…

I can't look away, either. Even as I accuse him of such a heinous crime, I'm drawn to that beautiful face like a moth to a flame, knowing that I'll burn up for this guy for just the chance to get close to him.

"I… you're going to kill him. Is that right? That grave… the one that we… it's for *Max*?"

"That's the plan."

And he knew that all along, didn't he?

"There isn't anything I won't do for you, Sally," he murmurs. "He hurt you. I hurt him. I'll hurt anyone who goes after you… I promised, didn't I? You wanted no one to hurt you. I'm just doing what you want."

Is that how he justifies it?

I don't understand. I want to… I want to *desperately*, but why this? Why *me*?

Just—

"Why?"

"Because I love you."

He says it as simply as if telling me it's Halloween or that it's nippy out. Like it's an understandable fact, and he's kind of surprised I don't already know that.

I didn't.

Part of me warns that I need to shove him away, putting some distance between us. The other part? She moves closer, brushing my lower belly against his obvious erection as I whisper, "You don't know me."

Behind us, Max makes another noise.

Hunter doesn't let go of me. Instead, tucking me under his arm, he guides me over to where Max is unable to find a way to get to his feet. With his hands tied, his feet tied, his body immobilized and his mouth probably in agony, he's rocking back and forth, close enough to the grave that he's about to fall in… and he interrupted my conversation with Hunter.

He doesn't seem to like that.

This kick goes straight to Max's arm, the *crack* splitting through the dark night's sky, followed by more muffled grunts coming from behind the blood-soaked gag.

Then, as though he hadn't just broken my ex's arm, he turns to me. "I made it my mission to learn everything about you. Not my twin. *Me*. From following you around town, watching you from outside of your window, guarding your fire escape… this might be your first night with me, little doe, but it's not my first night with *you*."

For a moment, I completely forget about Max.

"You've been stalking me?"

More than that when you put together everything he knows about me…

"Watching you," Hunter corrects. "Making sure no one hurts you. You didn't know it yet, but you were mine from that first night."

"But… you never went to the café." The man I got to know myself, that I thought was Hunter Reed… "That was your brother."

"That was Hunter," he corrects. "It was just Nicholas getting to be him so that you… you could get to know *me*."

All of this must make sense to him.

Me? Not so much.

"Hunter… I don't understand."

"I loved you enough to keep you away from my dark side. From my obsession. From my all-consuming need for my innocent little doe. That's why I watched you, but I stayed in the shadows. Nicholas… his Hunter could be the man you deserve, but fuck it, baby. We both know he's not what you *want*, is he?"

I... I don't know. I was attracted to the Hunter who came for his coffee every time I was working, but the masked man who hungers for me... who needs my body like he needs a breath of air... who mutilated my ex for talking shit about me?

I should be screaming myself, running away like one of those idiot heroines in old horror films. Looking back would be my downfall, and yet...

I turn so I'm looking up at Hunter again, keeping my back to Max.

If I don't see him, he's not there...

"Hunter— *oh*."

I wasn't expecting that. The moment I shifted toward Hunter, he slipped his hand beneath my skirt. He finds my pussy easily, rumbling deep in his chest when he sees that—despite what's going on right now —I'm soaking fucking wet.

He dips one finger inside of my entrance, cutting me off from what I was about to say with the perfect distraction.

He works a second one in there while placing his hand on the small of my back, forcing me to arch it, showing my ass off to my ex as my Halloween lover starts to fuck me with his fingers.

I don't stop him.

I *can't.*

And I'm barely listening to him until I hear him say, "But now? I'm a bad man, Sally. A selfish man. I didn't want to bring you into my world of shadows...

but you're here now. You're a part of me," he says, using his thumb to flick my clit, "just like I'll be a part of you long after tonight's over."

My hands are on his shoulders now. I've gone up on the tippy-toes of my flats, giving him full access to my pussy. My skirt covers his hand so even if Max is coherent enough to know what's going on right in front of him, he can't see shit.

I'm panting softly, trying to make sense of what Hunter just said.

Long after tonight is over…

That makes it sound like he still plans on us only having tonight. That doesn't make sense to me, not after his confession of love—and obsession—and I just about squeak out, "Are you going to let me go?"

He crooks a finger. A rush of pleasure has my knees going weak, and I fall into him completely.

He drops his mouth to my ear. "You promised me 'til midnight, little doe."

That's not an answer—and not technically the truth, either—and I… I don't care.

"Come back with me to the cabin," I plead, moving my hips so that I can take more of his fingers, riding his hand. "It's warm there. There's a bed. We can spend the rest of Halloween there together."

I like that idea.

Hunter?

He withdraws his fingers, pulling his hand away from the heat of my pussy.

Gazing down on me, he says, "Are you asking me to spare him?"

I didn't say that.

With a thumb slick with my cream, he strokes my cheek. "He hurt you. He has to die."

"Hunter…"

"He won't be the first. Probably won't be the last, either. But for you… I told you. There isn't anything I won't do for you."

Wait a moment…

"Who else did you do this to?"

"Not just like this, but there was a creep. A fucking pedo who thought you were younger than you are. I caught him trying to sneak up your fire escape. Believe me, baby, he didn't get that far…"

And I never knew because I had Hunter Reed watching over me from the shadows.

"Oh."

He smirks. God, I fucking love it when he smirks.

"Does it turn you on to know I've killed for you?" he asks. "Let's find out."

His hand goes back under my skirt. Trailing two fingers through my slit, he murmurs, "Fuck" under his breath before taking his hand back.

Shit. I think I might be even wetter than before— and he knows it.

"It does," he says, using the hand on my back to shift me just enough that he could reach for his zipper. "I can't leave my sweet Sally like this."

"Hunter—"

He hoists me up, ordering me to wrap my legs around his waist as he cups my ass with both hands.

His cock is already out, nudging the entrance to my pussy. I'm so damn wet, he can't just push himself inside of me. Holding me in place with one hand, he grabs his shaft by the base with the other, angling it where it belongs, then groans as he slides home.

I stiffen, not because the intrusion is unwelcome or unpleasant, but because Max is still *right there*.

Hunter knows what I'm thinking, too.

"Let him watch," he says, as though it's some great magnanimous act before he inevitably kills my ex. "Let him see what he threw away. Let him know that I'll *never* make that fucking mistake."

He pulls his hips back, withdrawing halfway, then thrusts back into me.

I gasp, and he grins.

"That's it. That's my good girl. Forget about him. Just look at me."

I can do that, though it's hard when I see the love and possession and *need* screwing up his features as he fucks me.

Hunter says he loves me. I think he loves the *idea* of me... but can't I say the same thing about him? He's insistent that the man I spent four months slowly falling for is him, even though it really was his twin, but if Nicholas acted as Hunter...

That's it. I've officially lost it because, right now, this all kinda makes sense to me.

I pant his name—*Hunter*—and hold on tight as I'm riding his cock instead of his hand now.

Consumed by this man, it's easy to forget what's going on around me. I know that's why he's doing this. That Max's fate was sealed the moment he walked onto Reed property. Even if I did ask Hunter to spare him, I'm not so sure he would… but while he's showing me what he's capable of, he's also making sure I know he's doing this all for me.

In between pumping into me and dropping his face to suck on my neck, Hunter's right side jerks.

My eyes fly open in time to look down and see that Hunter has kicked Max flat to his back.

My ex lands with a thump and a scream muffled behind his gag, trying to roll away from both Hunter and the waiting grave.

That's when Hunter lowers us to the ground, never once breaking the connection of our bodies or stumbling in his frantic yet smooth strokes as he has me sitting on his lap, facing him.

It happens so fast after that. If I hadn't gasped, opening my eyes at just the wrong—*right*—moment, I don't know if I would've seen it happen.

Hunter's on his knees now, arm beneath my skirt as he wraps it around my back, keeping me on his lap as he moves his hips, thrusting up into me.

His hand slashes downward, going right for Max's throat.

He hits some kind of artery with the first strike. Hot blood sprays all over me, my dress, my hair. Max is gurgling, Hunter softly grunting as his body owns mine.

Another slash, this one opening up a gash in Max's throat. This time, the blood seeps out, shining in the moonlight.

Hunter drops his knife while never, ever letting go of me. Hands back to my ass, he lifts us both back up, then kicks again.

Max's body lands with a thump in the grave right about the time Hunter reaches beneath my skirt again, bloody fingers slipping between our bodies as he pinches my clit and I climax just as my ex dies.

I'M... NUMB.

I don't know how to feel, so feeling nothing at all seems like the right idea.

Max is lying on his side at the bottom of the grave. There's a gaping hole in his throat, blood staining his skin, white hoodie, and probably the blanket under his body. I can't tell, though. It's a deep red blanket so it hides it pretty well.

Hunter is standing at my back, adjusting my dress

so that I'm covered. His chin rests on the top of my head, his hands gliding up my sides once he's done.

Five minutes ago, he was fucking me while Max gargled and died.

Five minutes ago, I lost myself to my pleasure while thinking, "He's right. Max deserves it."

And now… now I'm standing here, the wind whipping the body of my dress, trying to avoid the vivid red dots that will eventually brown that managed to get all over the skirt.

I'm standing here, and with Hunter supporting my back, my body nearly boneless from how quickly he just used me, I'm just *numb*.

He squeezes my upper arms. It doesn't hurt—because, damn it, Hunter… both Hunters… they promised not to hurt me—but the touch is enough to draw my attention away from the corpse of my ex.

"Don't fear me, little doe. Everyone in this fucking town is afraid of Hunter Reed… except for you. You weren't. I did this for you… but I don't think I can take it if you're afraid of me now."

Am I afraid? He's used that knife on me twice tonight: to cut off my panties, then when he sliced me enough to draw blood that he lapped up like a kitten.

I wasn't afraid. All along… I've never been *afraid*. I used the thrill of the chase to feel invigorated, getting off on the idea that this crazy bastard wants me so badly that he'll run all night, *chase* all night, just to have the chance to fuck me.

But this was supposed to be about sex, right? Even when my gorgeous customer—whoever he was at the time—was pulling me in, putting me under his spell, offering me one night with him on Halloween, I knew it would end with the most amazing sex I've ever had.

And it has.

Murder, though?

Slaughter?

Hunter slit Max's throat and kicked him into a prepared grave without missing a stroke as I clung to him, panting nonsense in his ears.

And, with all of these other gravestones around us, I have to wonder how many other times he's spent his Halloween night just like this.

What was it Kelsey told me? That she'd heard screaming at the Reed House on Halloween before?

So did I, and I still... I'm still not ready to leave.

What does that say about me? Who knows. But if I'm being honest with myself... maybe I don't feel numb, seeing Max at the bottom of that grave.

Maybe I feel relieved—and vindicated.

And I admit, "I'm not afraid. I just... this isn't what I was expecting."

"It had to be done," he says simply, rubbing the back of my arms with his thumbs. "You'll see. And, believe me, Sally, you have nothing to fear from me. That's what I do to people I don't like. Who deserve to be hunted. That's not you."

I want to believe him.

Is it insane that I kinda *do?*

Shuddering, shivering, I rip my gaze away from the grave. Turning into Hunter, bracing my hands against his chest, I tilt my head back and ask, "What about people you do like?"

His blue eyes darken. "Let's get one thing straight: I don't like. I love with a fire more intense than you'd find in any of the jack o'lanterns in town. I obsess. I need. I *hunt,* but I make it fair enough. You agreed to the game. You agreed to the terms. If you get out of the graves before midnight, you'll never see me again—"

I suck in a breath. After tonight… why does the idea that this is it hurt me more than anything else?

Exhaling softly, I remind him, "And I get four grand."

"You'll get the money regardless for giving me the chase I've always needed. That's my twin handling that. But you and me, little doe… if you don't escape—"

This time, I gulp. "I'm yours."

He doesn't answer—and that's an answer in and of itself.

"For how long?" I ask. "One more night. One more Halloween?"

His hands had moved to my shoulders. Now, he ghosts them over up the sides of my throat, stopping when his fingers cup my cheeks, his thumbs touching the edge of my jaw.

"Oh, little doe. You have no idea what kind of monster you're toying with."

I remember the grave behind me. "I think I do."

"You knew my terms. If I catch you, I fuck you. You catch me, you get whatever you want. If you stay… I won't let you go, Sally, but trust me… you'll never want to leave."

That's the question right there.

Do I *want* to?

Letting go of me, Hunter takes one pointed step back. He dips his hand into his back pocket, pulling out a phone.

He shows me the screen.

"It's 9:40. You have a little over two hours to make it out—or to decide you won't want to."

I could go right now. I'm pretty sure I could find that gate again with plenty of time to spare. I just… I'm not sure I'm going to.

But when Hunter's gorgeous face becomes a daring smirk before he orders, "Run," I'm helpless to obey.

So I run, unsure if I'm running from him—or to a world I never knew existed before this Halloween.

COME OUT, COME OUT,
little doe...

11:57 PM

HUNTER

It's close to midnight, and I'm standing on the other side of the gate, waiting for the next few minutes to pass.

I've been here for almost an hour. As soon as I let Sally go again, I thought about shoveling the dirt on top of her worthless ex. The sense of satisfaction I get after a kill always lingers as I cover up my handiwork, but I usually wait for Nicholas to grab a shovel of his own and join me.

He was busy, then. Distracted. That meant the grave would have to wait, and without him watching the gate for me, I wouldn't know if Sally dashed right for it if I wasn't already there, ready to intercept her.

I was careful not to let her know I trailed her. It surprised me when she veered off to the right, heading in the opposite direction of the gate. My little doe would need to be able to scale a tree or suddenly grow an extra two feet to even attempt to leave our land by climbing over the eight-foot-high, iron-wrought fence that protects our property.

No. If she wanted to leave, she needed to do so through the open gate… and, so far, she hasn't.

Nicholas is back in the shadows with me, purposely keeping out of sight, hiding in the darkness so that Sally won't see him when she inevitably approaches the gate.

He left his car in the garage after he came back with our target, then disappeared into the house for a while with his latest Tamryn knock-off. That was three hours ago and he only just joined me about fifteen minutes ago in case I needed him.

I can only guess how the rest of his night went. His hair is wet, his clothes changed, and his cologne wafts over to me on the breeze. My twin obviously took a shower, but that's not surprising. Once he gets off, the first thing he does is scrub the other women off of him because, even if they look like his Tam, they don't smell like her.

I did ask him if he needed me to dig another grave. He shook his head before he backed into the shadows so at least I know this one survived her night with Nicholas.

There's still no sign of Sally yet.

Where the fuck is she?

The leaves beneath our feet rustle as Nicholas edges closer. He keeps to the side, still hidden, but he's near enough that I can hear his low voice carry over to me.

"Birthday's almost over," my twin notes. "You enjoy your present?"

Our birthday might be almost over. That means Halloween is, too, but my time with Sally?

Never.

My eyes stare unblinkingly ahead, watching the path for some sign of her. Only when I scowl, stamping my boots against the dirt when I still can't catch the moon glancing off her short blonde hair, do I finally say, "Yeah."

"Do you think she'll stay?"

Good fucking question. "I want her to."

"What if she doesn't?" asks Nicholas. "I know you said you'd let her go—"

"I lied."

The noise Nicholas makes in the back of his throat tells me all I need to know: he guessed as much, and if I decide to keep Sally, he'll be the one to turn the lock on her himself.

My hand twitches, itching to reach for my knife. I would never use it on my twin, and I'd kill myself before I ever hurt Sally, but I'm wound up so damn tight, I need a release. I'd hoped to find it with my girl, but more than that... I just want to pick her up, lick her clean, and drop her in my bed where I can keep her for as long as possible.

But I can't do that if I don't know where she is—and it's 11:58 now.

"Fuck! Where is she?"

"I'm right here."

Goddamn it. How did I miss her? With her soft steps and delicate form, I looked away long enough that she was able to sneak up on me.

How much of that did she hear?

Sally is wearing her blood-spattered dress, her white flats covered in dirt, and she's nibbling on her bottom lip as she approaches the open gate.

As if on cue, Nicholas nods at me. I catch the gesture out of the corner of my eye before he's gone again—and now it's just my little doe and me.

She stops on the other side of the gate, firmly on Reed land.

I'm not a gambler. If I play a game, I only do it if I know I'm going to win. And if I'm not sure, I don't gamble—I *cheat*. That's just how I'm wired. I'm a fucking Reed. I do what I want. I *take* what I want.

But when it comes to Sally Clark… I stayed away for months because her safety was more important to me than my obsession. Nicholas gave her to me for one night. I'm the one who was playing for forever—and, suddenly, I'm not playing at all.

I'm going to take it, one way or another.

Sally knows it, too.

Staying just out of my reach, she starts the conversation by reminding me, "You said if I can't escape you, I'm yours. Forever."

I did say that. I also know that she believed I was full of shit when I said it—just like how she purposely looked anywhere but at me when I told her I loved her in front of her ex before I went for his throat.

"You ready to leave?"

If she miraculously makes her way past me, Nicholas won't let her get past *him*.

"No. I mean… not yet." She tilts her chin a little, firming her delectable little body as she says, "I found you."

Technically, I was waiting for her. But if she wants to say that she did… "And?"

"The rules of your game, Hunter. If I found you, you'll give me what I want."

Without looking away from Sally, I tell her honestly, "It was never just a game for me. I thought you would've figured that out by now."

I'm not being fair. From the moment she stepped foot onto my property, she believed this was a one-night thing, and it was just because one of her customers was willing to pay her a good amount to spend the night together. Even I didn't know what exactly *Hunter* had in store, but I knew one thing that Sally didn't:

That she was the most tempting prey I've ever

chased, and there isn't anything a man like me won't do to keep it forever.

But if she still thinks this is a game… Sure. I'll play a little longer. "Forget that. What is it you want me to do?"

"Answer a question," she says quickly, almost blurting it out. "Honestly."

"Ask it."

"Before… when Max was there. You said you loved me."

I wait for her to add anything else. When she doesn't, I offer her a smirk. "Where's the question in there?"

"Did you mean it? That you love me?"

Is that all she wants to know?

Love… this is the closest to love as I'm ever going to get. She owns my thoughts. She owns my loyalty. That one smile… I'd kill a hundred fuckers just to have Sally look up at me through the fringe of her dark eyelashes—such a contrast to her pale hair—and simply *smile* at me.

After tonight, there's no doubt she owns my cock.

So love?

"Yeah. I meant it as much as a man like me can."

"A man like you… because you kill people. Right?"

Close enough.

"Yes."

"Bad people?" she said, the hopeful tone obvious.

I don't want to crush her, but I won't lie to her, either. "Sometimes. That prick I killed tonight was a piece of shit. The bastard who thought he could sneak in through your window? He deserved what he got. But sometimes… sometimes good people have to die and it can't be avoided."

Sally gulps. "Like me?"

"*Never.*"

I would never let anyone hurt my sweet Sally. Neither would Nicholas, not because he really cares about her, but because he knows *I* do—and he would never hurt me.

"But I know your secret. What if I told?"

She could try. I'm sure there have been plenty of witnesses who ran to the Shadowvale police about my family over the years, but it doesn't matter. I could probably walk down Main Street itself, stab a guy, and all it would do was add to my reputation.

"Go ahead. It doesn't matter to me. Even if they believed you, nothing would happen. Think about it. You came up to the Reed House. You stayed out at night. You fucked Hunter Reed—"

"I broke the rules."

Fuck that.

Moving into her, I lift my hand, cupping her chin, angling her head back so that she has nowhere else to look but at me.

"We make the rules, little doe."

Her lips part on a whisper of a sigh, her big brown eyes begging me to kiss her.

I oblige.

When Sally digs her fingers into my shirt, clutching me, pulling me closer as I keep her in place, taking her with my mouth, I know that I have her. Anytime she even mentions leaving me in the future, a forceful kiss should be enough to remind her who she belongs to.

Her fingers are twisted in the fabric as she pulls away, panting slightly. I allow it only because she's keeping the connection, and I'm not ready to release her chin.

"Is it midnight yet?" she asks.

My phone's in my pocket. I have no fucking idea what the exact time is, but I lie and say, "I think there's maybe a minute left," because, more than anything, I want Sally to choose me. To choose this.

If she wants money, she can have it. I've paid more for pussy less worthy than hers. To have her as mine… it's priceless.

"Tell me, Hunter. Be honest. If I walked out that gate right now, would there be a grave for me?"

Honest? I've never lied to Sally, and I won't start now. "No. But there would be a cage."

"A… a cage?"

"A gilded one," I assure her. "If you're mine, I'll give you whatever the fuck you want. Money? It's yours. A car that won't crap out on you first chance it gets? Done. Staying with me means *staying with me.* No more shithole apartment. You'll live here, and I won't stop until I've fucked you on every inch of my land."

"But why? I'm not the first girl to spend Halloween up here… so why me?"

Wasn't she listening when I answered her question before?

"Because I've been fucking obsessed since the moment I saw your haunted eyes and retail smile that night outside the coffee shop. Everyone else crosses the road to avoid a Reed at night, but you? You smiled, then you let me walk you home. How could I not fall for you? Or fall fucking harder and harder the more I learned about you since?"

"But that was your twin—"

"That was Hunter," I say firmly.

Sally doesn't understand. Not entirely, and not yet.

She will, though. She'll learn that, whether it was Nicholas or me who was the Hunter she developed feelings for, it's me who will do anything to keep her.

I bow my head, pressing my forehead against hers for a moment.

"If you choose to stay, you'll be the finest trophy I own, little doe. My most prized hunt." I pinch her chin, not even to hurt, but to get her lips to fall open again in a quick gasp. I swoop in, sucking her tongue into my mouth, then nip on her bottom lip before stroking the underside of her jaw. "Mine for this Halloween and every night that follows."

Even as she clings to me, I can see the doubt lingering in her big doe eyes. She doesn't believe me. That I love her, or that I'll take care of her.

That's okay.

She *will*.

And when she purposely keeps her feet planted on Reed land long after it becomes midnight on November 1st, I grin even more wickedly than the skeleton on my ruined mask ever did.

Because my sweet Sally, my little doe, my *forever* just turned the lock on her cage herself—and we both know it.

Happy fucking Halloween indeed.

CLOSE TO MIDNIGHT

AUTHOR'S NOTE

Thanks for reading *Close to Midnight*!

While this is a standalone, it is a part of a duet. As I mentioned earlier, Nicholas will get a novella next—and you'll get to meet the mysterious Tamryn!

I also want to let you know that, if you purchase a physical copy of this book—paperback, discreet paperback or hardcover—please send me your name and mailing address via email (carinhart-books@gmail.com) and I'll mail you a free *Close to Midnight* bookmark and a signed bookplate!

And don't forget to keep reading because I have the cover and a sneak peek of the follow-up book in this series—*Really Should Stay*—right now :)

xoxo,
Carin

REALLY SHOULD STAY

A SNEAK PEEK AT CHRISTMAS WITH NICHOLAS AND MISS CARLISLE

NICHOLAS

She's blonde. Long, slightly wavy hair spills across the deep red satin sheets, but it's a soft yellow color instead of a deep chestnut brown.

If she's meant for me… what the fuck kind of present is this?

Hunter's the one who usually goes for blondes. The first time I went to Thanks a Latte, being him, I wasn't surprised to see that Sally had platinum hair in a pixie cut. Her impish expression, big doe eyes, and petite build were just the sort of features that have my twin creaming his pants.

Me? Before I met Tam, I didn't have a preference. She was the fifth partner I ever had—after Mindy Lopez when I was fifteen, then Sophie Woodrow and Jasmine Johnson when I was sixteen, and Cara Maine the summer before I started my junior year—and each of my previous lovers was different than the last. The only thing they had in common was a wet cunt, a pretty face, and they were more than happy to let a Reed twin do whatever the hell he wanted to them until I grew bored and moved on.

But then I met Tamryn Carlisle.

Every single woman I've fucked since then has tanned skin, dark brown hair, and bright brown eyes.

So why did Hunter bring a blonde home for Christmas?

Leaving her in my red room was a given. The rest of Reed House is off-limits to anyone who isn't family —except for this particular room on the main floor. It's down the hall from the back entrance, making it easy for me to lead my escorts straight to this space. That's all they're allowed to see. There's even a bathroom for them to wash up in after I'm done with them, and a quick boot out the door before I take my own shower in the master bath of my main bedroom.

Sally's the first woman Hunter ever fucked indoors. I already knew he was keeping her, and that, when she didn't walk through the open gate at the end of our property even after watching Hunter slit her bastard of an ex's throat, she was happy to be kept. But when he shuffled her into my car, instructing me to drive us back to the front of the house as if I was his goddamn chauffeur or something, then carried her over the threshold like she was his fucking bride, it took everything I had not to pat myself on the back.

I did this. *Me.* Just because I couldn't have the one woman I wanted, that didn't mean my twin couldn't. So I became Hunter for months, drinking enough of that nasty coffee shit to make my piss stink like the stuff, and made the girl fall in love with him.

Then I gave her to him for our birthday, and she never left. She loves Hunter even more now that she knows who the real one is, and every time I hear her pant his name when I'm walking down the hall to my bedroom in the same wing where theirs is, I have to smirk.

To say I have a God complex is downplaying how fucking amazing I am. With a snap of my fingers, I can sentence a man to death. With a look at my twin, I can watch the light go out of our target's eyes after Hunter delivers the killing blow. With a whim, I can affect half the population of Shadowvale; as the CEO and owner of the sawmill and sanitation company that employs half the town, they need me.

They *worship* me.

I *am* God.

I have money. Power. The looks, and when I play the part, the charm. I have everything a thirty-year-old man could ever want… except for *her*.

And that's why I can't do this. A blonde? Hunter gave me a blonde?

There must be something about her that my twin thought would satisfy my specific needs.

The eyes, maybe? The slight tilt to her nose?

Freckles?

Something.

Closing the door behind me, sure that I'll be heading back out again in a moment, I stride across the carpet, reaching the single king-size bed in the center of the room.

Her breathing is slow and even. Her impressive tits catch my eye, and I wonder if that's why Hunter thought she would do… until my gaze jerks a little higher and the heart I swore I didn't have fucking *stops.*

No. That's not true. How can it be? For all the blood in my body to shoot straight to my cock, the useless organ has to beat.

So it does and, suddenly, I'm a seventeen-year-old idiot with a hard-on for the first-year English teacher I just can't get out of my fucking head.

Now I'm eighteen, doing every fucking thing I can to catch her attention now that I'm not her student any longer. I'm of age, a senior at Shadowvale, and have Mr. Braden for English that year. Bumping into her in the halls, joining the drama club because she's the advisor, even walking her to the car like I'm a gentleman instead of fantasizing about taking her in the backseat.

I'm turning nineteen, I graduated last June, and

the night I did, I fucked Miss Carlisle for the first time. That entire summer, while she was off and could pretend that she wasn't a teacher, I didn't use to be her student, that we're just two young kids in love— until that Halloween night when I showed her my love was unconditional, and the Christmas Eve after when I learned hers *wasn't*.

My body, finally getting over the shock of seeing her lying there, finally catches up completely to my eyes.

Now I'm thirty with another hard-on for the former English teacher who I've never been able to get out of my goddamn head.

But while she's stuck in my brain, Miss Carlisle— with a head of blonde hair instead of the brown I knew so well—is in my favorite bed. She's tied up, her body gift-wrapped just for me…

My hands clench into tight fists as a thought slams into my brain; lust wars with jealousy, and jealousy fucking *wins*. After taking one last look at my sleeping beauty, then adjusting the throbbing erection behind my suit pants, I promise her I'll be right back, then stalk toward my door.

When he's obsessed with the one who got away…so his twin gifts him to her for Christmas.

NICHOLAS

There are only two people in this world that I've ever cared about: my twin… and *her*.

Tamryn.

Miss Carlisle.

My English teacher when I was in high school—and the woman I couldn't stay away from, even when she told me I should.

Even when all of Shadowvale thought I should…

as if I cared about that. Still, I did what was expected of me. I didn't pursue her until after I graduated. Then, after the fateful Halloween when I turned nineteen, I claimed her as mine—but, by Christmas, she was *gone*.

I didn't chase. That's always been Hunter's thing, and he tried to find her for me. I know he did.

What I didn't know? Was that he never stopped searching—just like I never stopped thinking of Tamryn of mine.

So when Hunter one-ups last year's birthday gift to him by leaving Tamryn next to my Christmas tree this year, there's no doubt in mind about what I'm going to do with her.

Anything I *want*.

TAMRYN

I made it a little over two years as a teacher before scandal had me changing my name, changing my looks, and walking away from the biggest mistake I ever made.

Eleven years later, I have to admit that *leaving* was a bigger one.

Nicholas Reed. I knew what I was getting into when I went to his house that Halloween, but I thought it was okay. He was the one he pursued me, and he wasn't my student anymore.

No. But when he killed my ex in front of me, then

expected me to look past it, I knew that he was more trouble than I needed—especially when I end up being the cops' only suspect in Logan's murder.

I kept my silence about what Nicholas did, and, in exchange, he kept his distance. But as the years slipped by, I couldn't help but think I saw him there. Over my shoulder, in the reflection of a storefront window, even in my gated community.

But it wasn't Nicholas, was it? It was his twin—and he's finally decided it's time I go where I belong.

It's time I return to Shadowvale and face the man Nicholas has become, and who I'm still inexplicably drawn to a decade after I saw him last... even after he makes me a deal that I can't afford to refuse.

Really Should Stay is a standalone dark romance novella that is set on Christmas Eve/Christmas Day and can be read all year round! It tells the story of one half of the ruthless Reed twins, and the one woman he'll do anything to have... again.

Out now!

door sex scenes, profanity, on-page death, and a HEA that is perfect for the characters... well, the ones that *survive*, that is.

KEEP IN TOUCH

Stay tuned for what's coming up next! Follow me at any of these places—or sign up for my newsletter—for news, promotions, upcoming releases, and more:

CarinHart.com
Carin's Newsletter
Carin's Signed Book Store

facebook.com/carinhartbooks
amazon.com/author/carinhart
instagram.com/carinhartbooks

ALSO BY CARIN HART

Deal with the Devil series

No One Has To Know *standalone

Silhouette *standalone

The Devil's Bargain

The Devil's Bride *newsletter exclusive

The Devil's Playground

Dragonfly

Dance with the Devil

Ride with the Devil

Reed Twins

Close to Midnight

Really Should Stay

Standalone

My Wife